Bofuri ★ I Don't Want to Get Hurt, so I'll Max Out My Defense.

MAPLE

Maple's STATS

Lv24	HP 100/100
MP 22/22	
[STR 0]	[VIT 236]
[AGI 0]	[DEX 0]
[INT 0]	

Skills

Shield Attack, Si...
Taunt
HP Boost (S...
Great Shiel...
Absolute D...
Hydra E...

Welcome to
NewWorld Online.

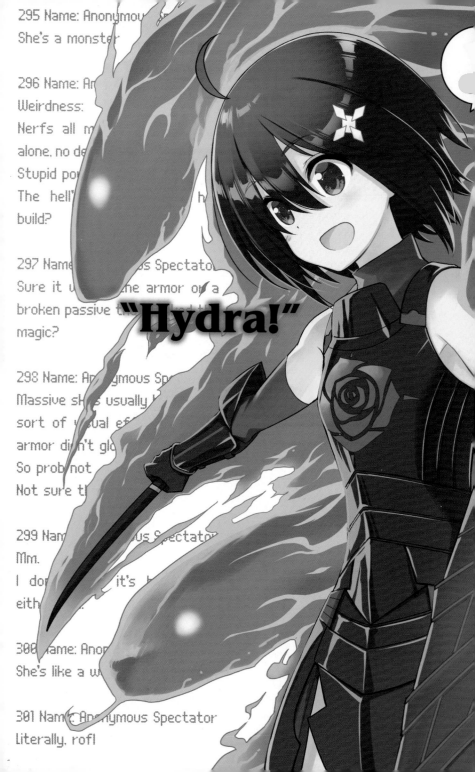

295 Name: Anonymous Sp...
She's a monster

296 Name: An...
Weirdness:
Nerfs all m...
alone, no de...
Stupid po...
The hell'... h...
build?

297 Name... s Spectato...
Sure it u... he armor on a
broken passive t...
magic?

"Hydra!"

298 Name: Anonymous Sp...
Massive sh... s usually...
sort of visual ef...
armor didn't glo...
So prob not...
Not sure t...

299 Nam... us Spectator
Mm.
I do... it's...
eith...

300 Name: Anon...
She's like a w...

301 Name: Anonymous Spectator
Literally, rofl

A purple magic circle appeared on her blade, and light of the same color poured forth.

The Battle Royale

The cool breeze carried the scent of sunflowers and the sea. Listening closely, they could hear waves lapping against the shore.

"Wow..."

"You definitely don't get to see this every day."

Bofuri
★ I Don't ★ Want to Get Hurt, so I'll Max Out My Defense.

①

YUUMIKAN

Illustration by **KOIN**

YEN ON
NEW YORK

Welcome to
NewWorld Online.

Bofuri I Don't Want to Get Hurt, so I'll Max Out My Defense.

YUUMIKAN

Translation by Andrew Cunningham • Cover art by KOIN

ITAINO WA IYA NANODE BOGYORYOKU NI KYOKUFURI SHITAITO OMOIMASU. Vol. 1
©Yuumikan, Koin 2017
First published in Japan in 2017 by KADOKAWA CORPORATION, Tokyo.
English translation rights arranged with KADOKAWA CORPORATION, Tokyo, through TUTTLE-MORI AGENCY, INC., Tokyo.

English translation © 2021 by Yen Press, LLC

Yen On
150 West 30th Street, 19th Floor
New York, NY 10001

Visit us at yenpress.com • facebook.com/yenpress • twitter.com/yenpress
yenpress.tumblr.com • instagram.com/yenpress

First Yen On Edition: March 2021

Yen On is an imprint of Yen Press, LLC.
The Yen On name and logo are trademarks of Yen Press, LLC.

Library of Congress Cataloging-in-Publication Data
Names: Yuumikan, author. I Koin, illustrator. I Cunningham, Andrew, 1979– translator.
Title: Bofuri, I don't want to get hurt, so I'll max out my defense / Yuumikan ; illustration by Koin ; translated by Andrew Cunningham.
Other titles: Itai no wa Iya nano de bōgyoryoku ni kyokufuri shitai to omoimasu. English
Description: First Yen On edition. I New York : Yen On, 2021–
Identifiers: LCCN 2020055872 I ISBN 9781975322731 (v. 1 ; trade paperback)
Subjects: LCSH: Video gamers—Fiction. I Virtual reality—Fiction. I GSAFD: Science fiction.
Classification: LCC PL874.I46 I8313 2021 I DDC 895.63/6—dc23
LC record available at https://lccn.loc.gov/2020055872

ISBNs: 978-1-9753-2273-1 (paperback)
        978-1-9753-2274-8 (ebook)

10 9 8 7 6 5 4 3 2 1

LSC-C

Printed in the United States of America

CONTENTS

I Don't Want to Get Hurt,
so I'll Max Out My Defense.

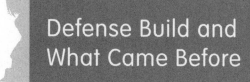

Defense Build and What Came Before

"Hmm...I haven't really played many games," Kaede Honjou said with a sigh, gazing at the box art of a new video game. Her friend Risa Shiromine had insisted she take it. "And I always end up doing whatever Risa says..."

The cover showed several characters holding swords and staves, topped with a colorful logo that read: *NewWorld Online*.

VRMMO games like this one were all the rage these days. Even Kaede owned the VR console required to play them. Not that she'd used it much. It was collecting dust in her closet.

She only owned it because Risa—again—had talked her into it.

"*Sigh...* I can never say no to her..."

Kaede was holding a note from Risa that listed all the instructions on how to get started.

"When she looks at me with those puppy-dog eyes, I lose all will to resist."

Risa had been convinced Kaede would play the game. Not playing would definitely leave Kaede feeling guilty.

"Might as well...! Guess I'll run through basic setup."

Kaede dusted off the machine and fired it up.

It wasn't like she had anything against games.

And if she had someone to play with...

With that in mind, Kaede started the game up.

◆☐◆☐◆☐◆☐◆

Armed with Risa's instructions, Kaede got through *NewWorld Online*'s initial setup easily enough.

"Whew...I guess that's it."

She was ready to dive into the virtual world. It had been a while since Kaede last experienced this sensation. She closed her eyes, and when she opened them again, she was in the game. But not in a town or anything; she still had a little setup left to go.

"First...a name? Hmm. Well, I don't want to just use my real name, so...let me see..."

She thought for a minute and decided to use the English name for the tree she was named after. She typed *Maple* and hit CON-FIRM. The panel hovering in front of her changed, prompting her to choose her starter equipment.

"Greatswords and one-handed swords. Maces and staves. Hmm... I'm not really great at running around, and I don't want to get hit a lot... Maybe I should pick staves and be a mage?"

She flicked through more options until she found one that seemed perfect for her.

"Great shield and short sword? Not much attack—but the highest defense? Oh! As long as I have super-high defense, I won't take any damage!"

Convinced by the tutorial text, she finalized her starting gear selection.

Great shields were not a common first choice among most

players. Raising defense only negated damage in the very early game, and most people agreed that pouring points into DPS was more worth it.

And not many people picked their starter gear based on the assumption that they were going to get hit a lot. Plus, there were plenty of shields that could be equipped with a one-handed sword or a mace—just not a great shield.

Since those options offered more flexibility, they were far more popular.

"Next, my stat points... I guess I better put them all into Vitality."

This was a very one-sided build. Put bluntly, she was min-maxing her stats. Great shields already left her with low attack, and putting no points into Strength only exacerbated that shortfall. Plus, since she was ignoring Agility, she wouldn't receive any speed boosts, meaning she could only move as fast as she did in real life.

And how many people could honestly claim that they naturally moved faster than a charging beast?

"Oh...I can't adjust my height? I wanted to be taller."

Kaede was only four-foot-nine. She was slim, cute as a button, and more popular at school than she realized. But however much she might want to change things, discrepancies between a player's height and build in the real and virtual worlds often detracted from the experience, so she was forced to abandon the idea.

"Okay. I think I'm ready! Let's do this."

Her body was enveloped in light.

And when she opened her eyes again, she found herself standing in the middle of a bustling village.

CHAPTER 1

Defense Build and First Battle

Kaede—now Maple—looked around, taking in the sights of the game's first town. She was standing in a square with a fountain and several benches. The square was connected to the main road, which was paved with stone and flanked by brick buildings. There were players walking all around. The sky above was a brilliant, clear blue, and the sunlight made the water in the fountain sparkle.

"Where am I…? Menu time!"

There was a hum, and a transparent blue panel appeared in the air in front of her.

Maple

Lv1 HP 40/40 MP 12/12

[STR 0 〈+9〉] [VIT 100 〈+28〉]
[AGI 0] [DEX 0]
[INT 0]

Equipment

Head	[None]	Body	[None]
R. Hand	[Starter Short Sword]	L. Hand	[Starter Great Shield]
Legs	[None]	Feet	[None]
Accessories	[None]		
	[None]		
	[None]		

Skills

None

"Hmm…VIT is Vitality, right? I'm pretty sure that's defense. Have I messed up already?"

Maple hadn't played a lot of games, but it didn't take much imagination to realize that a bunch of zeros in her stats was *bad.*

Looking back at her life in general, she couldn't really remember *any* positive zeros.

She went through her skills one by one. Thanks to her weapon, her Strength wasn't actually zero, but she had no Intelligence, Agility, or Dexterity.

"Ah-ha-ha…that isn't good. What now? Risa isn't here to help me…"

She thought about it for several minutes, then decided she would at least try fighting a monster. If that didn't work out, she could always start over.

"Okay, time to leave town!"

Maple began walking toward the town exit.

Everyone else is moving…really fast, she thought.

When she'd been standing still, she hadn't realized how big an impact AGI: 0 had.

But she didn't let it get her down. She kept going until she reached the field outside.

Time for her first battle.

The town's outskirts weren't as crowded as the square, but there were still people around. Fighting here would mean someone was bound to see what Maple was up to.

"If this goes badly, I'd rather not have an audience… Let's walk a little farther."

Maple kept trudging along until she was deep in a nearby forest. There was no sign of anyone else in the area.

"This looks as good a place as any other… All right, monsters! Come at me!"

It wasn't clear if it was specifically because of her invitation, but a white rabbit with some sharp horns came running out of the grass. It charged her at fairly high velocity. With no speed boosts at all, could she dodge the bunny's attack? Absolutely not.

"Hey! Whoops, sorry!"

Even Maple wasn't sure what she was apologizing for. She hastily tried to raise her great shield but didn't quite make it in time, and the charging bunny nailed her right in the stomach.

"Oof! Wait…that didn't hurt!"

The bunny's attack should have scored a critical hit, but instead, it did no damage at all. Confused, it backed away.

"Wow! This is great! It didn't hurt at all! I guess that's what VIT: 128 can do for you! Heh-heh-heh. Well, Mr. Bunny? How do you like my abs?"

Maple flexed her torso with a flourish, though she didn't have much of a six-pack to show off. It was a little on the soft side, even.

The bunny seemed to take her exposed belly as a taunt, or maybe it was programmed to only do one thing—either way, it charged her again.

Maple weathered the hit with her body alone, not even raising her shield.

The bunny charged again and again while Maple simply stood there chuckling. Occasionally, she ran after it, goofing around. She even tried to pet it.

If anyone had seen this happening, they would've shared it on the forums immediately.

Playing tag with a monster was odd enough, but the sight of Maple laughing with her hands on her hips as a bunny relentlessly lunged at her—that was post-worthy.

Their battle—if it could be called that—went on for a full hour. Maple was laughing happily the whole time, having too much fun to notice how much time had passed.

"Come on—you can do better!"

But as she taunted the bunny again, she heard a voice in her mind.

"Skill: Absolute Defense acquired."

"Hmm? What's this? …Give me a second, Mr. Bunny." Entirely unconcerned by the charging monster, Maple started checking out her new skill.

Skill: Absolute Defense

Doubles the user's VIT. Raising STR, AGI, or INT requires 3x more points.

Condition

Be attacked for one hour without taking damage or doing any damage with spells or weapons.

"Uh…seems like my Vitality is two hundred and fifty-six now. Also, this skill sounds amazing! And here I was, just playing with a bunny."

Maple thought this skill was easy to acquire, but an ordinary great shielder wouldn't have enough defense. Figuring it would cause problems later, virtually nobody put all their starting points into Vitality. And even if they did, it was unlikely that they would want to spend over an hour messing around with a bunny.

In other words, it was a nigh miraculous series of decisions that had granted her this skill. As a result, Maple was the only player who had it.

But Maple herself remained cheerily oblivious to this fact.

"Okay, thanks for waiting… Mr. Bunny?"

"Squeak…"

Each time the bunny charged, the impact knocked it back to the ground, causing damage. Over its head, there was an HP bar…

…and it had just gone from red…to nothing.

The sound of something shattering rang out right before the rabbit vanished without a trace in a cloud of light particles. It didn't even leave an item behind.

"Mr. Bunnyyyyyyyyyyyyyyyyy!"

"You are now level two."

* * *

"Mr. Bunnyyyyyyyyyyyyyyyy!"

Maple's wail echoed through the quiet forest.

◆□◆□◆□◆□◆

"Awww...why did you have to die? I wasn't even trying to kill you..."

Maple lamented the bunny's demise for a while, but eventually, she recovered enough to check out the results of her level-up.

"Oh! I got five more points to spend on stats!"

With these points, she could say good-bye to that row of zeros.

"Hmm...but raising anything besides Vitality now seems like a waste."

Once spent, there was no getting these points back. Maple had to make them count.

"Okay! My mind's made up! Vitality it is!"

Maple put all five points into VIT, then set off without a second thought to find another monster.

Given that monsters found deeper in the forest were both stronger and more numerous, it was not surprising that Maple didn't have long before she encountered another one.

"Ewww...so gross..."

A giant centipede had wrapped itself around her ankle. Surely, there was no one alive who would describe that as anything but gross.

Maple drew the short sword from her hip and stabbed at the monster's body. The centipede was poisonous and injected venom with each bite, but since every attack had failed to penetrate Maple's skin, it had been unable to inflict any status effects on her.

Very much unlike the bunny, the centipede was not cute at all. Maple had no interest in goofing around with this monster.

She had no qualms about defeating it.

Sadly, her DPS was so low, she had to stab it a full ten times before it died.

"Seems like I didn't level up this time..."

Maple considered turning back. She wasn't the type to lose herself in the joys of grinding, so her main takeaway was that fighting centipedes took an excruciatingly long time. She wondered if she should try looking for some weaker monsters.

Unfortunately, Maple had already ventured too far into the woods, unknowingly stumbling into the area where the strongest monsters lived.

And in a stroke of terrible luck—one of these monsters had just found her.

A Giant Bee, wings abuzz, hurtled right at Maple.

"Augh! Don't!" she yelled, raising her great shield in an attempt to ward off the bee's terrifyingly large stinger.

But with AGI: 0, she was no match for the Giant Bee's speed.

Before she knew it, the bee was on her back, stabbing at her neck—at least that's what she thought was happening. The flying monster was certainly attacking her, but it was no match for her defense. Maple took no damage!

The Giant Bee kept trying to sting her anyway.

"Ah-ha-ha! That tickles!"

Maple had recovered from her initial fright and had quickly regained her usual good cheer.

After several more unsuccessful attempts, the bee must have decided stinging was pointless. Instead, it tried a different tactic—one that involved spraying venom.

"Hngg...?!"

It didn't hurt much, but Maple definitely felt a mild burn, almost like getting in the bath with a sunburn.

She checked her status screen and saw that her HP had only gone down by one. Apparently, this poison was a type of damage Maple couldn't completely nullify. If she was poisoned like this another thirty-nine times, she would die.

"…………Time for a strategic retreat!"

Maple turned and began running away. But the discrepancy in their Agility stats made this impossible.

The Giant Bee kept spitting out poison, and Maple failed to dodge any of it.

"Agh…"

Maple was now at half health.

"Skill: Poison Resist (S) acquired."

As soon as she heard those words, Maple stopped taking damage. She would normally have been delighted—but not this time. She was too preoccupied with her mild annoyance that this Giant Bee had actually succeeded in hurting her. This was the very first time she took any damage!

"I'm done for…," she lamented as she collapsed on the ground, making a show of feebly crawling away.

She was *acting*. Maybe the bee believed her performance, maybe it was just a coincidence—either way, the bee reacted just as Maple had hoped.

It started really laying on the venom, like it had her on the ropes. As Maple continued feigning her deteriorating condition, the bee seemed ready to finish her off with one final spray.

*   *   *

"Skill: Poison Resist (S) has evolved to Poison Resist (M)."

Maple grinned. This had been her goal. A flawless triumph over the only weakness she had discovered thus far.

Maple stopped moving at all, playing dead. Seeing that she was no longer struggling, the bee began charging a powerful attack. It moved closer to her face, ready to feed.

"Heh-heh! Gotcha!" Maple cried. She flipped over, sword in hand, and stabbed the bee right in its open mouth. The soft flesh within its maw offered no resistance as her blade popped out the back of the monster's head.

Maple twisted her sword, gouging right and left. The HP bar above the bee's head began slowly shrinking.

The bee frantically stabbed at her with its stinger, but this proved futile.

After a few final shivers, the Giant Bee turned into motes of light.

A silver ring appeared in the space the bee had previously occupied and fell to the ground.

"Heh-heh-heh... I win!"

"Skill: Giant Killing acquired. You are now level eight."

Maple picked up the ring and decided to investigate it alongside her new skills.

Forest Queen Bee Ring [Rare]

[VIT +6]
Autoheal: 10% of Max HP every ten minutes.

---

*   *   *

"Ohhhh! This is great! HP recovery! And it's rare? How lucky!"

Considering how Maple still had the MP of a brand-new character and hadn't yet learned any spells, a recovery item was an enormous boon. It also boosted her Vitality by six points, which was a nice bonus. And since she had the Absolute Defense skill, that became a twelve-point boost.

She took off one of the gloves she'd started with and slipped the ring on. The gloves were just cosmetic items that didn't enhance any stats, so she put it back on over the ring.

"Risa's note did say that if I got any rare items or skills, I should keep them secret."

The main concern was Player Killers, but of course, it would be very difficult for anyone to kill Maple now.

"What about these skills…?"

Poison Resist (M)

Nullifies strong poison.

Condition

Sustain strong poison attacks forty times.

"Huh…it didn't seem *that* strong. But maybe my VIT was reducing the poison damage…"

Her hunch was correct. She would have taken much more damage otherwise.

But without a resist skill, poison attacks did a minimum of one HP.

"Next!"

Giant Killing

If four or more stats (other than HP/MP) are below those of your opponent, double all stats (except HP/MP).

Condition

Solo kill a monster while four or more of your stats (other than HP/MP) are less than half the enemy's respective stats.

"I've got four stats at zero, so…that means my stats will be doubled in almost every fight! And my VIT will be quadrupled!"

Maple was right. Since her other stats were all zero, the only thing this skill did was double her Vitality. This made it very easy for her to activate and incredibly useful for her specialized build.

Moreover, the level-up had given her some more stat points to spend.

"Huh, I only got fifteen stat points… I wonder if you only get more on even numbers…"

This time, Maple didn't hesitate. She put every point she had into VIT.

Given the nature of Giant Killing, this was the best move.

Maple's VIT stat was now at a whopping 616.

"Hmm… I'm kinda tired. Maybe I should call it for the day. This took more time than I expected…"

Maple emerged from the forest as she returned to town, where she wandered the streets a little bit before finally logging out and returning to the real world.

CHAPTER 2

Defense Build and Concentration

"Okay! Let's roll out!"

Maple had logged in to *NewWorld Online* to pick up where she had left off the previous day.

"I think I'll hit up the forest again. I could use some more skills!"

Maple was particularly eager to grind levels, but acquiring new skills had been undeniably exciting. It was like filling an empty bookshelf.

"The more skills I get that raise VIT, the better!"

Maple set off from town, winding her way back to the forest—still very slowly.

"What should I try today?"

The first thing she thought of was enemy detection. If she could sense enemies approaching, it would be insanely useful.

"All right, time to get cracking!"

Maple rested her shield on the ground, closed her eyes, and searched for signs of enemies.

This approach…was completely misguided.

The proven method was already documented on the strategy forums. Players could use bows or thrown rocks to hit unseen, nearby enemies like they knew exactly where they were. Any number of players had successfully done so.

Besides, if Maple's approach succeeded, it would be because she could do the same thing in real life.

Maple was not psychic.

Blissfully unaware of this, Maple kept her eyes closed, focusing very hard.

She did this for three whole hours. At this point, she was basically asleep.

The source of this tenacity was an eternal mystery, but what finally pulled Maple out of her trance was a system message.

"Skill: Meditation acquired."

"Mm? Huh? Meditation? Not Enemy Detection? That's a little disappointing…"

Maple tried to get up, only to discover an unexpected weight keeping her from rising. She opened her eyes and found herself covered in centipedes, caterpillars, and other weak monsters—though there was also a scary-looking wolf ready to attack her.

"Aiiiieeeeeeeeeeee!"

She shrieked and began slashing wildly with her short sword. With STR: 9, freeing herself took a while. The monsters simply refused to die. But however feeble Maple was, none of them could harm her at all, so she was able to stab to her heart's content.

Things might have gone easier if she only had to deal with the enemies that had been clustered around her, but unfortunately, Maple's shrieks were attracting the attention of one new monster after another.

"Skill: Taunt acquired."

New skills were always good, but what she really needed was a way to get out of this predicament.

Eventually...

"You are now level eleven."

"Whew...that was a hard fight. Better check out these skills!"

Meditation

When active, recover 1% of Max HP every ten seconds.
Effect lasts ten minutes. Consumes no MP.
Unable to attack while Meditation is active.

Condition

Meditate for three hours while under attack.

"I wasn't meditating, though...but this skill seems really strong, so I'll take it!"
She moved on to Taunt.

Taunt

Draw the attention of all monsters. Has a cooldown of three minutes.

Condition

Gather the attention of ten or more monsters at the same time. Item usage permitted.

"That sounds useful for grinding levels."

This skill was usually used by parties to make their enemies focus on the player with the highest defense, but this didn't immediately occur to Maple. A more pressing concern for her was that her low AGI would leave her chasing impotently after enemies who could easily run away. She was likely the only player in the game who had ever needed to worry about this.

Either way, this skill meant she would have no problems grinding.

"Now I just have to put all my stat points in VIT... Huh? I have ten stat points?"

Yes, every ten levels gained would come with twice the usual amount of stat points. This was a common game mechanic, but to Maple, it was an unexpected gift. She was delighted.

Maple

Lv11   HP 40/40   MP 12/12

[STR 0 ⟨+9⟩]   [VIT 130 ⟨+34⟩]
[AGI 0]   [DEX 0]
[INT 0]

Equipment

Head	[None]	Body	[None]
R. Hand	[Starter Short Sword]	L. Hand	[Starter Great Shield]
Legs	[None]	Feet	[None]
Accessories	[Forest Queen Bee Ring]		
	[None]		
	[None]		

Skills

Taunt, Meditation, Poison Resist (M), Giant Killing, Absolute Defense

Maple finished scrolling through the status menus, nodded happily, and logged out.

Meanwhile, an online forum was heating up.

[NWO] I saw a crazy great shielder!

1 Name: Anonymous Greatsworder
Crazy

2 Name: Anonymous Spear Master
Deets

3 Name: Anonymous Mage
Crazy how

4 Name: Anonymous Greatsworder
She was hanging out by the west forest with like, a dozen centipedes and caterpillars swarming her.

5 Name: Anonymous Spear Master
Huh? No way.
She'd like, die instantly. Great shield or not.

6 Name: Anonymous Archer
^ This
She have good gear? Explain.

7 Name: Anonymous Greatsworder
Looked like starter gear.
Getting grossed out just remembering.
There were literally bugs everywhere, and she was totally cool with it.

8 Name: Anonymous Mage
If that didn't kill her, then she must have negated all the damage, right?

9 Name: Anonymous Spear Master
Is that doable?

10 Name: Anonymous Archer
Iirc during the beta, a full defense build could soak the white rabbit's attack.

11 Name: Anonymous Spear Master
Those are trash, though.

12 Name: Anonymous Great Shielder
I think I know her

13 Name: Anonymous Greatsworder
Tell us more

14 Name: Anonymous Great Shielder
Dunno the player name, but cute girl, like 4'9" tops.
Walk speed suggests AGI is basically zero.
Also if I tried what she did I'd melt in no time flat.

15 Name: Anonymous Mage
So it's an extreme min-max build? Maybe she stumbled on a hidden skill?

16 Name: Anonymous Spear Master
That would explain it. But is it true she's insanely cute?

17 Name: Anonymous Archer
That's what you honed in on?
Same tho.

18 Name: Anonymous Greatsworder
Hmm, guess we gotta dig for more intel.
If she becomes a top player, we'll know soon enough.

19 Name: Anonymous Great Shielder
I see anything else, I'll post.

20 Name: Anonymous Mage
Any and all updates are appreciated! o7

And thus, Maple quickly became a hot topic someplace she would never visit.

◆□◆□◆□◆□◆

"Here I am again..."

This was Maple's third day in a row logging in. She'd originally started this to play with Risa only to very quickly become totally addicted to the game itself.

The twin joys of acquiring new skills and steadily raising her defense to ever greater heights proved compulsive, compelling her to boot up her system despite herself.

Risa's parents had ordered her to study, and she definitely wasn't supposed to be playing games instead.

"Heh-heh-heh... I'll just have fun on my own."

Maple was about to head out of town, but a quick look around made her realize something important.

"I'm...still wearing my starter equipment!"

A totally plain shield and a wimpy-looking sword. Some of the players she spotted were clearly elites wearing impressive, highly decorated equipment.

She spent a few minutes admiring everyone's outfits until she spotted a man carrying a very impressive great shield.

Maple walked slowly over to him.

"Ummm, where did you get that cool-looking shield?"

"Hmm? Uh, y-you mean me?"

The man had clearly not been expecting this interaction.

"Yeah! That great shield is really nice!"

"O-oh, well, thanks... It's a custom item. I paid a crafter to make it for me."

"Huh… I see…"

"Would you…like me to introduce you? I mean, we're both great shielders."

"Oh! Yes, please!"

"Then follow me."

It would have been perfectly reasonable to suspect some sort of trick, but Maple already had nothing but shields on her mind. It never even occurred to her to worry.

Fortunately for Maple, this stranger was just being nice.

In fact…

"Wow…I can't believe she spoke to *me*! I'll have to post about it later."

Turned out he was the Anonymous Great Shielder from the forum.

After walking for a bit, the two of them entered a shop.

Behind the counter just inside, a woman was working on something. When she heard them come in, she set her work down—and recognized one of their faces.

"Oh, welcome back, Chrome. What's up? Your shield shouldn't need maintenance yet."

"Nah, I just ran into a new great shielder and, uh…impulsively brought her here."

Maple stepped out from behind Chrome.

"Oh, aren't you cute?! And, Chrome, what impulses are we talking about here? Do I need to report this?"

The shopkeeper summoned a blue panel in the air in front of her.

"W-wait, don't! That was a slip of the tongue!"

"Heh-heh, I know. I'm just messin' with you."

"Whew…you almost gave me a heart attack."

Chrome looked very relieved.

"You shouldn't follow suspicious strangers," the shopkeeper warned.

"Erm…I know…"

"I'm not *that* suspicious!"

"Heh…well, enough chitchat. What brings you here?"

"She said she wanted a cool great shield, so I figured I should introduce her to you."

"Oh? Well, my name's Iz. As you can see, I'm a crafter—specifically, a blacksmith. I can do a little potion making, too."

"Oh? That's amazing! Oh, um. My name's Maple!"

Maple was slightly nervous. This was her first time meeting anyone in-game, and she had to work very hard not to trip over her own name.

"Nice to meet you, Maple. Why'd you pick great shields?"

"Um…I didn't want to get hurt, so I decided to focus on my defense."

"Hmm… I see, I see. You're going for a full VIT build? But… you don't have much money yet, right?"

Maple checked her funds. She hadn't bought anything yet, so she still had the starting 3,000 G.

"I-is three thousand G enough?" she asked, figuring it wasn't.

"Ha-ha…unfortunately not. You'll need at least a million. But you'll have that much before you know it."

This sounded like a dizzying amount of money to Maple.

"Erm…I guess I won't be fashionable for a while longer…"

"You could always give dungeons a try. They've got tons of treasure. That'll help you earn some money to boot, so why not give it a shot? No guarantees you'll find any great shields, though."

After getting some beginner advice, Maple added Chrome and Iz to her friends list so she could contact them whenever she wanted.

Then she bowed her head and left the shop.

Maple now had two goals—earning money and finding a dungeon.

"I hope there's some cool gear inside!"

---

241 Name: Anonymous Great Shielder
I ran into the great-shield girl and added her as a friend. lol.

242 Name: Anonymous Spear Master
Huh?

243 Name: Anonymous Archer
How?

244 Name: Anonymous Great Shielder
She logged in. looked around. made eye contact with me, and came running right up.

245 Name: Anonymous Spear Master
Super Social Shield Girl

246 Name: Anonymous Mage
What happened after?

247 Name: Anonymous Great Shielder
Asked me about cool shields.
Told her I'd introduce her to a crafter and she just straight-up followed me.

Her AGI's so low, she had trouble keeping up and I had to keep stopping to wait for her

248 Name: Anonymous Spear Master
How's your AGI?

249 Name: Anonymous Great Shielder
Hang on, lemme lay it all out
OK

Didn't form a party
Chose great shields 'cause she thought getting hit would hurt and she'd need defense
Super nice, outgoing

In short:
Hella good kid

The type you can't help but wanna help
Also I figure we'll need to trade info later so here's mine:
I'm going by Chrome in-game
My AGI's 20.
I wanna friend y'all so it'd be nice if we could all meet up by the fountain square at 22:00 tomorrow

250 Name: Anonymous Spear Master
Thanks for the intel—also, are you *the* Chrome?
You're a top player!

251 Name: Anonymous Mage
Waaay too famous. I'm kinda scared now lol

252 Name: Anonymous Archer
Cool. I can make that time.
But if you're leaving her in the dust at AGI: 20, she must have really
sunk every last point into VIT.

253 Name: Anonymous Greatsworder
We're gonna watch over her from now on too, right?

254 Name: Anonymous Spear Master
Totally!

255 Name: Anonymous Archer
Totally!

256 Name: Anonymous Mage
Totally!

257 Name: Anonymous Great Shielder
Totally!

Naturally, Maple had no idea this forum even existed.

CHAPTER 3

Defense Build and Dungeon Crawling

"A dungeon expedition! It's like I'm finally on a real adventure!"

Maple had spent her meager 3,000 G on potions, just in case.

She only had forty HP, so the most basic potions were plenty.

She also had the ring the bee dropped and Meditation. Still, if she was ever in a situation where she could take real damage, she would definitely be in trouble.

Maple decided she was as ready as she'd ever be and headed toward a dungeon she'd read about on a forum—the Poison Dragon's Labyrinth.

"I've got Poison Resist (M), so I should be fine!"

With that, she set off from town, excited about her first dungeon crawl.

Maple headed in the opposite direction from her usual forest haunt. If this wasn't a game and she wasn't carrying a great shield and short sword, a casual observer might have assumed she was on her way to a picnic.

Several monsters accosted her along the way, but since they couldn't damage her, she didn't even bother fighting them.

The monsters here seemed to be smarter than the ones in the forest, so once they realized they couldn't harm her, they all ran away.

Nobody saw any of this, so Maple's freakish defense went unnoticed.

As she pressed on, the trees she encountered were progressively more withered while the ground was cracked and dry. The landscape felt increasingly desolate.

She even passed by a number of bubbling swamps.

After ten more minutes, she came upon a rise in the land, like the ground had cracked open its maw to swallow her whole.

"Is this it?"

Maple stepped inside and noticed the ceiling was much higher than she'd expected. She would have more than enough room to use her great shield here.

As she ventured deeper, some noxious-colored slimes and lizards came slithering along the ground and walls to swarm her.

"Hah! Take that!"

Maple stabbed a slime, but the core inside the gelatinous mass kept shifting around. Unable to land a clean hit, her attacks did no damage. But no matter how much the slime tackled her, it couldn't deal any damage, either.

"Hngg...this is getting me nowhere! How about this? Great Shield Smash!"

Maple raised her shield up and promptly fell directly on top of the slime, crushing it beneath her. This wasn't a real skill or anything, so there wasn't much power behind the move, and dropping to the ground right in front of her opponent left her badly exposed.

But however exposed she was, none of the monsters had any attacks or poisons that did Maple the slightest harm, so she wasn't worried.

The shield's impact didn't do much damage, but it was enough to crush the slime's core—exactly what she needed to kill them. Slimes turned out to be the perfect prey.

"Okay! Let's dive deeper!"

Now that she'd solved her slime problem, Maple tromped onward. She'd given up on the lizards. With Agility as low as hers, they just dodged every attack.

As she flopped on top of her shield again…

"Skill: Shield Attack acquired."

Maple quickly read the skill description. The name was sort of a dead giveaway, but it never hurt to be sure.

Shield Attack

Attack with a shield. Power derived from STR. Knockback (S).

Condition

Defeat fifteen monsters while landing the finishing blow with a shield.

"Not too useful…but that knockback could come in handy!"

Once she was ready, Maple kept going deeper. Given that it was a poison-themed dungeon, it was only natural for there to be all sorts of poisonous monsters…and traps.

Eventually, Maple reached a wide-open area. She'd been squeezing down narrow passages this whole time, so it immediately felt like she had entered a room. There were some flowers growing in the center—a nice little patch of color in the otherwise monotonous dungeon.

A few small purple flowers swaying side to side caught her attention.

"Those are cute... I wonder if they're an item?"

She moved closer, knelt down, and poked one with her finger. In response, the purple flower balled up like a bud and released a purple mist. This seemed to cause a chain reaction as all the flowers did the same thing. The mist was clearly poisonous.

"Whoa?!" Maple yelped. The whole room was becoming more purple by the minute. She got up and ran away.

She was quite a ways down the next corridor before she finally let out a sigh of relief.

"Th-that was close... I guess it makes sense that there *would* be traps."

Once she'd settled down, Maple started walking again—but the next open room contained a swamp that was clearly bad news. Some sort of gas was bubbling up from its murky depths.

"That's *obviously* poisonous. You can't fool me!"

Maple quickly decided to give it a wide berth as she moved past—when something flew out of the swamp and scored a clean hit on the back of her head!

"Augh! Wh-what was that?!"

After a moment scanning the area, Maple found what looked like a flying fish hopping around her feet.

"I-is this...?"

She glanced back at the poison swamp. This time she spotted a fish hopping out.

"That almost gave me a heart attack...," she groaned, carefully smashing the fish at her feet with her shield. She left the other fish in peace and continued on her way.

Avoiding monsters and traps while having a good time with all the slimes she encountered, Maple finally reached the end of the dungeon.

The double doors in front of her were three times her height.

She had to put her back into it to pry them open.

The unoiled hinges let out a shrill screech as they parted to reveal the room beyond.

There were patches of poison marsh dotting the ground, and the air itself was tinted purple.

As Maple tentatively stepped inside…

…the doors slammed shut behind her.

"Eep?!"

But the sound of her yelp was drowned out by the roar of the dragon rising from the swamp—and this wasn't just *any* dragon.

Its rotting, fetid flesh sloughed away, revealing the bones underneath. The monster had three long necks. Several eyes were missing, leaving only yawning gaps. When the dragon roared, it belched purple mist. The undead dragon from the poison swamp was far more intimidating than any monsters she'd met on the way.

"Th-this is the poison dragon?!"

Maple's alarm didn't seem to matter much to the dragon. It simply opened its three mouths and unleashed a torrent of toxic liquid at her. She raised her shield to protect herself, but the powerful poison-breath attack instantly enveloped her.

She'd closed her eyes, but upon hearing poison dripping on

the ground around her, she opened them again. Maple herself was unharmed, but her gear was not so lucky.

"M-my shield and sword…"

They were deteriorating, dissolving—and no longer remotely useful. Fortunately, she had a glove on over her ring, so that was safe.

But…

Maple's shield had provided +28 to her VIT, and thanks to the effects of Absolute Defense and Giant Killing, that number had been quadrupled—meaning she'd just lost 112 points of defense.

And that meant the poison dragon's breath could hurt her.

As things stood, each breath attack would deal three damage. And the first attack had already taken one HP from her.

Just thirteen more attacks and she was dead.

"Okay…focus! Meditate!"

Maple calmed herself, closed her eyes, and concentrated.

This time, she'd have to do it while enduring the pain of being attacked. Meditation's effect would only be active for however long she remained focused.

She had the ring and the Meditation skill, as well as the potions she'd purchased. Maple's goal was to use all of these in conjunction in an attempt to raise her Poison Resist. That was her only shot at winning.

While using Meditation, the pain and fear lessened. The sensations faded away, like her physical form was growing intangible.

This helped her persevere. Each time her HP fell below 20 percent, she drank a potion.

Over and over.

Her healing couldn't keep pace with the sheer amount of

damage. She would either run out of potions or gain the resistance she needed.

The outcome rested solely on which came first.

After she steeped in poison for quite some time, a voice echoed in her mind.

"Skill: Poison Resist (M) has evolved to Poison Resist (L)."

That's what Maple had been waiting for—but it was not cause for celebration.

Her skin was still burning.

The resist still wasn't strong enough.

Maple wasn't sure if the skill *could* evolve again, but she had to gamble on that chance.

Just as she drank her final potion...

"Ha-ha...I did it!"

The voice in her mind had announced that she'd acquired Poison Nullification.

Now the breath attacks almost felt pleasant.

But she couldn't just kick back and relax. As her HP recovered, Maple had to think.

Why? Because her weapon had been destroyed. How could she defeat this dragon? Its attacks couldn't harm her. But her attacks did no damage, either.

This was going nowhere.

Unless she died or defeated it, there was no way to leave the room. She could escape by logging out, but she'd gone to great pains to get this far; she wanted something to show for it. The developers most likely had not accounted for this particular stalemate.

"Hngg... Welp, I've just gotta start trying things! It's not like I have school tomorrow!"

Thankfully, it was the weekend. Maple could spend as much time here as she liked.

After a long process of trial and error, she finally hit upon a wild idea.

"The dragon flesh is all ragged and torn up...and since I can nullify poison, I bet I could eat it!"

She waded through the poison breath until she was right up next to the dragon.

And placed her palms together.

"...Bon appétit, I guess."

She took a bite of the dragon's back.

"Urgh...that's not very tasty," Maple said, making a face.

She experimented for a few moments and quickly confirmed that any flesh she swallowed would not regenerate. But if she merely tore some off with her teeth, those bits would eventually reappear—like a video rewinding. And of course, that did no damage.

"I guess I *have* to eat it..."

The poison dragon's flesh was slightly bitter. It reminded Maple of the green peppers she'd always detested.

But if she had to eat it to get out of the room, then she wasn't

going to stop, even if it meant holding her nose and biting back tears.

The one thing in Maple's favor was the fact that this game had no mechanic that made her feel full. Players could taste things, but no matter how much they ate, they'd never be stuffed.

"*Munch, munch...* Oh, Mr. Dragon! Thanks for breathing on me! *Chew, chew.* That adds a nice bit of spice. Kinda helps hide the green pepperiness."

She steadily worked toward the torso. After nearly five hours of eating, there was nothing left but bones.

Maple looked around, wondering if she should get started on the leftover tail only for all the bones to fall onto the ground as the whole thing stopped moving. Light appeared all around the dragon's corpse right before it vanished.

Having chewed all the way through a hole in the system's logic, Maple had finally defeated the dragon.

Where the dragon had been moments before, a glowing magic circle suddenly appeared—along with a treasure chest.

"Skill: Hydra Eater acquired. Subsequently, Poison Nullification has evolved to Hydra."

"You are now level eighteen."

Maple first spent her twenty new stat points on VIT.
Her base stat for VIT was now 150.

"Okay! I have even more defense!"
Next, she checked out her new skills. Maple had never expected there to be one called Hydra Eater.

Hydra Eater

Nullifies poison and paralysis status effects.

Condition

Defeat a poison dragon with HP Drain.

Apparently, eating monsters counted as an HP Drain. It seemed highly unlikely anyone but Maple had ever even tried this.

Technically, eating food *did* help HP recover a little.

That said, this was clearly not how the developers had intended for players to acquire the skill. The expected method was likely much, much easier. No one would subject themselves to eating a rotting dragon piece by piece if they had a choice.

Hydra

Allows free use of the poison dragon's power.
Grants the use of poison magic at the cost of MP.

Condition

Defeat a poison dragon with HP Drain after acquiring Poison Nullification.

Maple shivered with excitement.

"I finally have a decent way to attack! And poison? That's perfect for me!"

All she had to do was apply the status effect and wait. A very effective technique for a defense build.

"MP could be a problem...but I still want to spend all my points on VIT..."

She pondered this for a while but then remembered the treasure chest and put other thoughts aside.

The treasure chest was quite large. Nine feet wide, six feet deep, and three feet tall.

This was Maple's first treasure chest, and she gulped with anticipation. A wave of nervous excitement shot through her.

She slowly lifted the lid and peered inside.

"Ohhhhhhhhhhhhhhhhhhhhhhhhhhhhhhhh!"

Maple was so excited, her voice shot up.

Inside was a great shield. It was mostly black, with decorative red flourishes and a large red crystal embedded in the center.

There was also a set of armor, clearly designed to pair with the shield. It had an imposing gleam and a rose relief that wasn't too garish but still drew the eye.

Last was a pitch-black short sword, with a beautiful glittering garnet embedded in the scabbard.

"This...is...perfect! Ugh, it looks so cool!"

Maple quickly picked them up and read the descriptions.

Unique Series

One-of-a-kind equipment exclusive to the first player to solo a dungeon boss on their first attempt.
Only one per dungeon. This equipment may not be gifted.

Night's Facsimile

[VIT +20] [Destructive Growth]
Skill Slot: Empty

Black Rose Armor

[VIT +25] [Destructive Growth]
Skill Slot: Empty

New Moon

[VIT +15] [Destructive Growth]
Skill Slot: Empty

This armor was *only* for Maple. Even the short sword buffed VIT, throwing any idea of attacking out the window. If anyone besides Maple even tried to use this, they'd never be able to take advantage of it.

"I'll have to look up skill slots and Destructive Growth when I get back!"

Maple carefully put all three pieces into her inventory and stepped into the magic circle, which instantly transported her back to town.

As soon as she arrived, Maple spent her few remaining coins on a room for the night.

The game's inns allowed you to sleep in-game, but that wasn't Maple's goal today.

"First, I have to look those up."

Destructive Growth

When destroyed, this equipment is restored to its original form, growing stronger based on the damage taken. The repairs happen instantly and are not influenced by stats at the moment of destruction.

Skill Slot

You can sacrifice one of your skills, attaching it to a weapon.

Skills attached this way can never be recovered.

The attached skills can be activated five times per day at zero MP cost.

Additional usages beyond that require the standard MP.

You unlock one slot every fifteen levels.

"Heh-heh…these sound cool! And powerful!"

Certain she'd get more slots in the future, Maple didn't hesitate to pair Hydra with her short sword, New Moon. She wouldn't have to worry about her MP anymore.

"And now, the moment I've been waiting for—time to equip everything!"

Maple donned all her new gear and checked herself out in the mirror. She looked much more formidable than she had in her starter loadout, so Maple was thoroughly satisfied.

"Yessssssssssss! I look so good!"

She spent upward of an hour posing in the mirror. You know, getting used to her new equipment.

"Heh-heh-heh… Time to hit the town!"

Maple was acting like she was all dressed up with places to go, but she couldn't quite shake her nervousness.

And she was right to be nervous. This gear set drew even more attention than most top players—the aura radiating off it turned every head. Maple just failed to notice the majority of the looks she received.

It was getting pretty late, but Maple wanted to do one last hunt, so she set off once more.

CHAPTER 4

Defense Build and Secret Training

Covered in pitch-black armor, Maple sat on the edge of the fountain, worrying.

She wasn't making much progress with her level.

Maple was currently level 18, while the highest-level players were 48. Maple's initial lack of interest in the game had left her trailing badly behind the most active players. At this rate, the gulf between them was just going to keep growing.

So why was Maple struggling to level up? She didn't have enough Agility, so when she went out to grind, it was hard for her to reach places that were home to powerful foes.

"Hmm..."

Maple was scowling at an information board, scouring for some useful skills.

The reason she'd started taking this seriously was because the day before, the game company officially announced...an event.

In a week, there was going to be a battle royale where players would fight for points, awarded based on the number of players defeated as well as the number of deaths.

Total damage dealt and received would also affect the final score.

The top ten players would receive event-exclusive items as a reward.

"And when you hear the word *exclusive*, you can't help but want it."

Maple was the sort of person who would throw herself on top of a land mine if it said it was a limited-time offer. Those words were her one true weakness.

And that's why she was desperately searching for a way to close the gap between her and the top players.

"Hrngg... Guess I might as well try here!"

Maple stopped glaring at the information board and headed north.

Yes—Maple had *no idea*...

...how broken her defense really was.

"I've got tomorrow off, so I'm gonna sleep over and dig up some good skills!"

Maple had a sleeping bag in her inventory. This would allow her to safely sleep outdoors. It was a cheap consumable item, but diligently selling off the materials she had collected finally allowed her to start buying basic things.

Maple's gear was fantastic, but her wallet was painfully skinny.

After some traveling, Maple finally arrived at her destination: the northern forest.

Her sleepover hunt was primarily focused on two targets. One of these was the Exploding Ladybug—an insect notorious for running in close and blowing itself up.

The other was a classic foe found in many types of games—goblins.

"Okay... Taunt!"

A ring of light shot out from her, drawing in all the nearby monsters. Maple ignored everything but the goblins. There were five of those. The other monsters attacked her, but they did no damage, so she ignored them.

The goblins swung their rusty swords at Maple, but since they only attacked head-on and her shield was very large, Maple easily blocked their attacks, even with zero Agility. If she ducked her head down, the great shield covered nearly all of her.

She weathered the incoming blows and pushed back. And then she just kept doing that over and over again. There were five goblins, so it was five times as effective.

"Skill: Great Shield Mastery I acquired."

This was a core skill she'd read about online, so Maple had been expecting this.

It reduced incoming damage by 1 percent if she had a great shield equipped. She had realized she could raise her defense not just by pouring points into VIT but also by getting as many damage-reduction skills as possible.

"Taunt!"

Goblin reinforcements arrived, and having ten of them attacking all at once made her training even more effective.

Over the course of a few hours, Great Shield Mastery I evolved to Great Shield Mastery IV, and now all incoming damage was reduced by 4 percent.

She also acquired the Sidestep and Deflect skills. Each of these also reduced damage by 1 percent.

"I think that's good enough."

The goblins were still trying their best, so she brought things to a close by crushing them with her Shield Attack. Once was not enough, so she had to smash them with her shield several times.

"Skill: Moral Turpitude acquired."

Maple had not been aiming to acquire this skill.

Her play style was quite different from other players, and she spent long hours enduring things no regular player would bother with, so she kept getting skills nobody else would ever stumble across.

Moral Turpitude

Gain [VIT +1] each time you deliberately allow an enemy to attack you.
Effect lasts one day after the skill activates.
Max: [VIT +25].

Condition

Exceed the threshold for time spent deliberately allowing defeatable foes to attack you. Must not have received a death penalty before.

*   *   *

"Well, that was a happy accident!"

Resisting the urge to dance a jig, Maple headed farther into the woods.

For the first time since starting the game...

...Maple was *intentionally* seeking out an undiscovered skill.

As the name implied, Exploding Ladybugs were ladybugs that exploded. They were about twice the size of normal ladybugs. They offered little XP and lived deep in the forest, so it took ages to even find them. Additionally, since they were quite small, it was tough to dodge their attacks, but the damage they caused was considerable. Nobody else chose to hunt them—which meant Maple had the area all to herself.

When she reached the Exploding Ladybug zone, Maple used Taunt, drawing many of them toward her. Since nobody ever thinned the numbers, they were in plentiful supply. As the swarm flew toward her, Maple took New Moon and pulled just a bit of the blade from the scabbard.

"Paralyze Shout!" she said. Her volume was a bit low for something called a shout, but she accompanied it with a shrill scrape.

The skill she'd placed in New Moon's slot gave her access to all the poison dragon's skills, and the names of these had remained unchanged.

This unusual skill was activated by sound—and Maple used the sharp scrape of her short sword sliding back into its sheath as the trigger.

The reason she chose that was quite simple: She thought it was cool. Nothing more, nothing less.

Maple watched as the ladybugs fell to the ground, looking very pleased with herself.

Then she knelt down, closed her eyes...

...and started gobbling up all the bugs.

"Oh, they're like that candy that pops in your mouth! Not weird at all as long as I keep my eyes closed. I guess I already ate a poison dragon, so there's no point being picky now..."

Maple wasn't doing this without good reason.

And her theory was validated the moment she swallowed her fiftieth ladybug.

"Skill: Devour acquired."

"Skill: Bomb Eater acquired."

"Pretty sure that means I don't have to eat any more."

Maple brought up her new skills.

Devour

The power to eat anything and convert it to nourishment.
Converts spells, attacks, and items into MP.
Magic overcapacity is stored as magic crystals inside user's body.

Condition

Orally ingest a set amount of lethal substances.

Bomb Eater

Reduces explosive damage by 50%.

Condition

Defeat Explosive Ladybugs with HP Drain.

"Those are good skills! Ohhh, I'm so glad I forced myself to eat those bugs!"

Maple put Devour on Night's Facsimile.

Devour was always active, so there was no daily limit to worry about. And it could be used to consume attack magic or an enemy's weapon, rendering them powerless.

"And it'll convert those to magic crystals, letting me cast big spells with New Moon! Heh-heh-heh… That's so cool."

Maple struck a pose, like she was about to whip out her short sword. She'd clearly spent a lot of time practicing looking stylish.

"I was actually hoping to get explosion magic…but I like this, too!"

Now she just had to get her level as high as she could.

How would Maple do in her first event? She set off to continue grinding, looking forward to finding out.

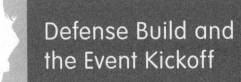

CHAPTER 5

Defense Build and the Event Kickoff

The day of the event arrived at last. Maple pulled up the blue panels to check out her final stats.

Maple

Lv20   HP 40/40   MP 12/12

[STR 0]   [VIT 160 〈+66〉]
[AGI 0]   [DEX 0]
[INT 0]

Equipment

Head	[None]	Body	[Black Rose Armor]
R. Hand	[New Moon: Hydra]	L. Hand	[Night's Facsimile: Devour]
Legs	[Black Rose Armor]	Feet	[Black Rose Armor]
Accessories	[Forest Queen Bee Ring]		
	[None]		
	[None]		

Skills

Shield Attack
Sidestep, Deflect, Meditation, Taunt
Great Shield Mastery IV
Absolute Defense, Moral Turpitude, Giant Killing, Hydra
Eater, Bomb Eater

"Okay! As ready as I'll ever be. Hope I don't take any damage!"

Maple had taken damage so infrequently that she was still unused to the sensation.

Plus, this would be her first time ever fighting other players. Naturally, she was a little nervous.

She waited at the starting square as a crowd of entrants gathered.

There was a giant display floating in the air. It would be livestreaming the actions of the most interesting players. The spectators were mainly crafters or players who'd decided not to join in.

"It's time for the inaugural event! Let the battle royale begin!"

A roar went up from the ground. Maple raised a hand, yelling, too—only a little embarrassed.

The announcement blasted over them.

"Allow me to explain the rules once more! The event will last three hours! The stage is a special map created just for this event! You'll be awarded points based on four factors: the number of enemies you defeat, the number of times you're defeated, damage dealt, and damage received! Total points will determine your rankings, and the top ten players will all get a special prize! Good luck, everyone!"

And with that, a countdown appeared on the screen. The moment it hit zero, Maple and the other participants were surrounded by light and whisked away.

"Uh...where am I?"
When the bright light faded, Maple opened her eyes.
She'd spawned in the center of a ruined plaza.
She glanced around quickly, but there was no one else there. Maple had been worried she'd have to fight immediately, so this was a relief.

"Well, even if I go looking for people, I'll never catch anyone... so I'll just wait here!"
Maple sat down on a large stone block and waited for another player to show up to attack her. She was relaxed but kept her shield at the ready.
She spent some time drawing in the dirt with a stick, until she heard noises around her.

They're here! she thought as she looked up, only to find someone already swinging a sword in her direction.

"Gotcha!"
Maple probably wouldn't have been able to block this attack in time before, but now she had Great Shield Mastery IV. Her body moved much more easily, and she handily intercepted the sword.

And swallowed it without a trace.

"Huh? A-aughhhhhh!"

Since the man's sword hadn't bounced off the shield, the momentum kept carrying his hand forward until it hit the shield, too. The moment he made contact, half his body was swallowed whole, leaving the rest of him to turn into particles and vanish. Since he'd lost his main weapon, it was entirely possible he'd just been put out of the fight entirely, sent to join the spectators. Even if he did have a spare weapon, he would find the rest of the event significantly harder.

And his life force became a pretty red crystal decorating the front of Maple's shield.

"I guess I'll draw some more!"

She picked up her stick again, for a second time leaving herself completely open to attack.

Maple was having so much fun drawing, she genuinely appeared to be full of openings. She wasn't *trying* to set a trap or anything, but this time she managed to hook a party of three.

Forming parties was not against the rules. They'd simply teamed up to try and get at least one of the party members into the top ten.

A man with a sword charged right at Maple. Just a beeline dash, no feints or tricks. But compared to Maple's AGI: 0, he was very fast indeed.

But closing a ten-yard gap still took much longer than the time Maple needed to make New Moon sing.

"Paralyze Shout!"

There was a shrill scrape, and all three players fell flat on their faces.

The red crystal on the shield shattered with a crack. Maple stood up, hoisting her great shield.

*   *   *

"Oh-ho…I win!"

This time, she just tapped the sword guy's head with the shield, avoiding his main weapons. The man vanished in a cloud of light particles.

Then she quickly dispatched the other two.

Each turned into a new red jewel, gleaming on the front of her shield.

"Great shields are way stronger than I thought!" she said, nodding happily. Things were definitely going her way.

She took a seat again, never once suspecting that she was the only great shielder who could do anything this ridiculous.

[NWO] First Event Spectators 3

241 Name: Anonymous Spectator
I figure Pain's gonna win it.
Highest level in the game, can't beat that.

242 Name: Anonymous Spectator
He's nuts.
Dude doesn't even move like a human anymore, lol.

243 Name: Anonymous Spectator
The people racking up wins are all famous already.

244 Name: Anonymous Spectator
The top players are superstrong, what a shock.

245 Name: Anonymous Spectator
Huh? What the hell? That's crazy!

246 Name: Anonymous Spectator
Everyone they show looks so strong.

247 Name: Anonymous Spectator
Provisional score ranks
Great shielder named Maple
120 kills, no damage taken

248 Name: Anonymous Spectator
Bwah?!

249 Name: Anonymous Spectator
Is she cheating? No...can't be...

250 Name: Anonymous Spectator
If she's racking up results like that, they gotta show her soon, right?

251 Name: Anonymous Spectator
Is that her now?

252 Name: Anonymous Spectator
Her shield! Just ate a sword lol!
wtf

253 Name: Anonymous Spectator
Cute face, gnarly play style
Between the status effects and that shield, nobody stands a chance

254 Name: Anonymous Spectator
So slow!
She's just countering their attacks.

255 Name: Anonymous Spectator
Yeah, moving like that, you'd normally get hurt.
I knew it, look, she's...huh?

256 Name: Anonymous Spectator
Huh?

257 Name: Anonymous Spectator
Huh?

258 Name: Anonymous Spectator
Did that greatsword just...bounce off her head?

259 Name: Anonymous Spectator
Is that like, even possible...?

260 Name: Anonymous Spectator
If it was, we'd all be doing it.

261 Name: Anonymous Spectator
The girl is more wild than the shield or that status effect.

Back in the event zone, Maple had finally gotten tired of sitting around and was currently trudging down a road.

There was a mob in front of her. More than fifty players had gathered together.

She'd seen a lot of parties, but none on this scale.

They were mostly mages, and the moment they saw Maple, they raised their staves and started casting.

They'd likely polished off any number of players who'd made the wrong turn down this road.

They were moving with practiced ease.

"Let's blow 'em away with magic!"
Her shield almost had too many crystals, making it more red than black. Maple was itching to use some.
She didn't need any more crystals, so she just face-tanked all fifty spells.
When their magic had run its course, Maple drew her short sword.
Her strongest attack required revealing the full length.
A purple magic circle appeared on her blade, and light of the same color poured forth.

"Hydra!"
A three-headed dragon made entirely of poison consumed every crystal on her shield, spewing an ocean of poison in all directions.
It took out the band of spellcasters and beyond, devastating every player in the vicinity.

----

295 Name: Anonymous Spectator
She's a monster

296 Name: Anonymous Spectator
Weirdness:
Nerfs all magic with VIT stat alone, no defense skills activated
Stupid powerful magic
The hell's going on with her build?

297 Name: Anonymous Spectator
Sure it wasn't the armor or a broken passive that tanked the magic?

298 Name: Anonymous Spectator
Massive skills usually have some sort of visual effect, but her armor didn't glow or anything
So prob not
Not sure tho

299 Name: Anonymous Spectator
Mm.
I don't think it's her armor either. Yet.

300 Name: Anonymous Spectator
She's like a walkin' fortress, lol

301 Name: Anonymous Spectator
Literally, rofl

There was only an hour left. This last leg of the event would decide the top ten.

Everyone braced themselves...

And an announcement blared.

"Current standings: Number one Pain! Number two Dread! Number three Maple! For the final hour, anyone who defeats these three will receive a third of their points! Their locations are all shown on your map! Good luck!"

"Guess they aren't letting me off easy," Pain said, not looking the slightest bit worried.

"Ugh, what a hassle," Dread said, rolling his eyes.

*　　*　　*

"Yay! Third place!" Maple said, delighted.

The event stream showed all three reactions, building hype for the grand finale.

And hordes of players rushed toward them, eager for a chance to take them out.

"There she is!"

A crowd rushed out of the forest.

Many of them had Agility to spare.

Maple couldn't keep up with their speed at all. A knife struck the back of her neck.

"Huh? Wh-what the hell?!"

But naturally, that didn't faze Maple.

The enemy player had been absolutely sure he'd landed a killing blow. Before he could recover his wits, the great shield ate him. Several more players flung themselves at her only to also wind up eaten even as they grumbled about their attacks not having any effect.

After seeing this happen a few times, the remaining players took a more cautious approach, slowly edging closer to Maple. Most of their attention was focused on the great shield and its instant-death attack.

These players had forgotten that Maple's main attack technique was actually her short sword.

"Fatal Poison Breath!"

Maple pulled New Moon halfway from its sheath, and a dense purple fog poured out.

*   *   *

"Paralyze Shout!"

Players in every direction hit the ground, unable to escape the lethal poison. The closer they were to her, the faster they turned to light.

Ultimately, all the players who dared to come near her were just added to Maple's score.

◆☐◆☐◆◆☐◆☐◆

"And that's all she wrote! Final top three remain unchanged! Let's proceed to the awards ceremony!"

The world in front of Maple turned white, and then moments later, she was back in the starting square.

The top three players were asked to take their places on the podium, so Maple stepped up to the third-ranked spot. There were a lot of eyes on her, and she found herself turning red.

And just as her nerves made her mind go totally blank, someone shoved a mic in her face.

"Next up is Maple! What do you have to say?"

The other two must have already spoken, but Maple had been too nervous to hear a word of it.

"Er, uh, huh? Um, I'm glad I had enough defenth."

Maple totally flubbed the last word.

Utterly blew it.

And she had no idea what she was being asked about, so her answer didn't make much sense to begin with.

*　　*　　*

Maple was too embarrassed to look ahead and never realized how many players were recording this.

She accepted her prize and made a beeline back to her room at the inn.

All night long, the forums were full of posts about how cute Maple was and theories about how she got so strong.

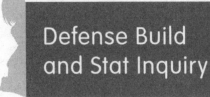

CHAPTER 6

Defense Build and Stat Inquiry

[NWO] The Mystery of Maple [An Inquiry]

1 Name: Anonymous Spear Master
A'ight, I started the thread

2 Name: Anonymous Greatsworder
Nice
The concern of the day is our precious little Maple

3 Name: Anonymous Mage
Honestly, she seemed even more nuts than Pain.
Why was she only third?

4 Name: Anonymous Spear Master
The girl spent most of the first hour doodling in a ruin

5 Name: Anonymous Archer
It was adorbs

6 Name: Anonymous Great Shielder
I'm starting to doubt that thing is even a great shield
I came in ninth btw

7 Name: Anonymous Spear Master
Noice
Getting that high with a great shield ain't easy
(Averts eyes from Maple)

8 Name: Anonymous Greatsworder
The final counts for Maple this time
Event 1
Maple: 3rd
Deaths: 0
Damage Taken: 0
Defeated: 2,028

Equipment includes a mystery great shield that swallowed enemies,
a short sword with ludicrously powerful status effect spells, and
black armor
The armor doesn't seem to be doing anything particularly OP
But her raw defense is so insane, she tanked spells from 50 mages
all at once without taking any damage.

9 Name: Anonymous Mage
No matter how many times I watch that, it's still insane.

10 Name: Anonymous Great Shielder
Great shield->Well, maybe there's gear like that out there somewhere?
Short sword->Yeah, again, maybe?
Maple herself->Huh?

Her stats and skill loadout are just a total enigma
How high is her VIT?

11 Name: Anonymous Greatsworder
She's literally a walking fortress
Literally

12 Name: Anonymous Archer
It did seem like she was tanking it all with just her VIT
Anybody have any idea what skills she might have?
When she was tanking those spells, there was a sparkly effect, so I
think there was definitely a skill involved

13 Name: Anonymous Great Shielder
Status effects->No clue
Defense boosts->If there were skills that made you that tanky I'd
have 'em
Great shield->Who knows

14 Name: Anonymous Mage
Yeah
We don't know a single one of Maple's skills, but I guess we can
assume she's got the basic ones.
It's the unique skills that are a mystery

15 Name: Anonymous Archer
She undefeatable one-on-one?

16 Name: Anonymous Mage
Serious possibility.
For starters, you'd have to do something about those AOE status effects.

She said "Fatal Poison" so that's gotta be a top-tier spell.
Which begs the question, where's her MP coming from?
She was slinging spells like crazy, but we all agree she's sunk all her points into VIT, right?
How does she have the MP for it?

17 Name: Anonymous Greatsworder
Yeah, I think that great shield is a magic reservoir
Seemed like everything it ate was turning into magic

18 Name: Anonymous Spear Master
So that's what the red crystals are?
They were shattering with every spell cast

19 Name: Anonymous Greatsworder
So basically Maple's build:
Maple herself has defense so high she doesn't take damage
But any attacks and players trying to bypass that get converted to MP
Then she slams 'em with status effects
QED

20 Name: Anonymous Spear Master
Is she the last boss

21 Name: Anonymous Archer
Yeah, one built by a real sadist

22 Name: Anonymous Great Shielder
And she might still have skills she hasn't shown yet

I mean, no one did any damage to her, so she might have like, auto-heals or whatever.

23 Name: Anonymous Mage
There oughtta be a law against final bosses that can heal

24 Name: Anonymous Greatsworder
I started laughing even as I was typing it up.
And she's only just started!
Rookie takes world by storm.

25 Name: Anonymous Mage
By the next event, she'll have something crazy on that armor, too!
Oh god

26 Name: Anonymous Archer
She's already a top player...
I'm doomed.
Perfect combo of cute and strong

27 Name: Anonymous Spear Master
Let's keep watch over her
She might have top-tier stats, but inside she's still a beginner.

28 Name: Anonymous Greatsworder
Good point.
Keep investigating however you can.

29 Name: Anonymous Archer
Roger that!

30 Name: Anonymous Mage
Roger that!

31 Name: Anonymous Spear Master
Roger that!

32 Name: Anonymous Great Shielder
Roger that!

The day after the first event, Maple was standing by the board, taking notes.

She was back to work finding damage-reduction skills and making a list of all known unlock conditions for such skills.

The three-month anniversary of the launch of *NewWorld Online* was only a day away. And to mark the occasion, there would be a massive update. It would add any number of new skills and items. The forums were abuzz with these, but they weren't the main attraction.

Everyone's top priority was a new map added in the update—accessible by defeating the boss in the northernmost dungeon on the current map.

The map was available whether you were solo or in a party.

Effectively speaking, this meant clearing the first zone to access the second.

Maple figured she'd give it a shot once she had a few more skills.

"Today I'm going for Great Defense!"

Maple was all fired up about it, but she soon discovered a problem. Night's Facsimile had a powerful skill that swallowed up everything. And the conditions for Great Defense required her to get hit a lot—which never happened, because she eliminated all threats before they hit her.

"Hmm…but with this shield, maybe I don't need that skill. Still…I'd prefer having a lot of skills…"

Maple thought for a while, but then she had an idea and set out once more.

"I hope this works…"

She was headed to where Chrome had taken her before—Iz's shop.

"Hey, you! Welcome back. You've sure made a name for yourself. To think you were still in starter gear the last time you came in!"

"Thank you! So…I have a favor to ask. Feel free to say no!"

With that preface, Maple started talking. When she was done, Iz nodded and summed it up to confirm the request.

"You want a new set of gear that's all white and nice-looking, but you aren't fussed about the stats. And you want to know how much that would cost? Well, if you bring in some materials yourself, I can do a set for a million G. Depending on the materials you bring me, it might end up with better core stats."

Night's Facsimile was a combat-oriented great shield—but not good for skill grinding.

So Maple had made up her mind to get a second shield expressly for that purpose—but the look of the shield was very important. She didn't want to just buy some crappy-looking spare. A lot of eyes were on her now, so she felt like she had an image to uphold.

She figured she might as well get a whole matching set.

Since her main set was pitch-black, her other set would be pure white.

Maple giggled at the thought. She could already see herself all dressed up.

"Got it!" she said. "I'll go get the money and materials!"

She dashed out of the shop.

And went back to the information board to find out where to get the materials she needed.

First, she needed pure-white materials that were hard enough. Maple found two materials that met those conditions.

The first were white crystals. Maple immediately realized that she could never gather these with DEX: 0.

So she headed out to gather the other option.

They were found in a large underground lake to the south of the town. The lake was rumored to be hiding secrets lying within its depths, but nobody had found anything like that yet.

Maple was looking for a kind of fish that swam in schools and had hard scales as white as snow. One fish in the school was the leader and so blue, it blended into the water.

"I read a story about that in grade school! It sure takes me back!"

Maple bought herself some fishing gear and set off for the lake in high spirits.

"Okay! Let's hook some fish!"

There was a small plop, and Maple waited for her first bite.

Twenty minutes passed.

"F-finally!"

Maple pulled the rod as hard as she could. The splash echoed across the underground lake.

She'd finally caught a white fish! It was flopping around behind her.

She left it there a minute, and then it disappeared in a burst of light, leaving a single two-inch scale behind.

Their actual scales were much smaller, but Maple told herself that's just how games worked and put it in her inventory. She had a lot more fishing to do, but tomorrow was a school day.

"I didn't think it would take *this* much time…hnggg… Okay, I guess I'll have to call it a day after two more."

Fishing also relied on your DEX and AGI stats, so Maple's fishing was incredibly inefficient. Crafters like Iz could probably catch a fish every minute.

Maple wasn't that lucky, so she did what she could and then logged out.

It would never do to sacrifice real life for the sake of a game. In that sense, she was much more levelheaded than the friend who'd invited her to this game, Risa.

"Whew…that's enough for today! Gotta get ready for tomorrow."

Kaede turned the system off, glanced over her schedule, and put the appropriate textbooks in her backpack.

"Okay! Good night."

She crawled into bed and was sound asleep a few minutes later.

Probably having wonderful dreams.

CHAPTER 7

Defense Build and a Friend

"Okay! I'm outta here!"

Kaede headed off to school, in uniform.

The sun had been getting warmer the last few days, and it felt great. Like spring had finally arrived.

Kaede's seat was in the window row, and with this sunlight streaming in, she would fall asleep if she let her guard down for a second. Risa sat two rows over, and she would definitely be sleeping through the afternoon.

Wondering if there was any way to prevent that, Kaede made her way to school. She lived close by, so she always walked in—and the walk only took five minutes.

There was a nice breeze, and the walk was easy enough.

Kaede had never had hay fever, so she loved spring unreservedly.

"All right! Let's make it a good one!"

She went through the school gates, walked into her class, and sat down in her seat.

Previously, she'd passed the time reading, but since she started playing *NewWorld Online*, she often spent the time thinking about new skills instead. It was always fun imagining what skills might be out there and what the conditions might be.

"What're you grinning about?"

Someone bumped Kaede on the head.

She looked up and found Risa smirking at her.

"N-nothing!"

"*Really?* Oh, right, that's not why I came over. Ahem...hee-hee-hee. Kaede, your attention please! I have a major announcement."

Risa leaned over, moving conspiratorially close. The dramatic throat clear and weirdly pompous tone in the back half were definitely getting Kaede's attention. She adopted the same tone.

"Hmm? What news, Risa? You seem unusually excited today."

"Glad you asked! I have *finally* been granted permission to play games once more!"

Kaede offered a round of applause.

Risa must have really applied herself to her studies. Her beaming smile proved all the hard work had paid off. Just seeing it made Kaede happy for her.

"I pushed you into getting the game and then kept you waiting for quite a while! But today I can finally join you!"

"Then we can form a party!"

"That we can. Wait...you already started?" Risa was so surprised, her voice jumped up.

Fortunately, they'd both shown up early, and there was no one else here. They didn't need to worry about drawing attention to themselves.

"Yeah...ah-ha-ha."

"You. Kaede. The same girl who only grudgingly agreed when I made you buy the game."

"You noticed?!"

"I'm thrilled! I didn't think you'd ever play it on your own! But you're all in?!"

Risa leaned in closer.

"What level are you? Or did you just make an account and call it a day?"

"Er, um...I'm...level twenty..."

Risa's jaw dropped. Then the full implications dawned on her, and a grin spread ear to ear.

"Wooow... You got way more into this than I ever expected!"

"Hngg..."

Kaede glared up at her, turning red. Risa savored this a moment, but she wasn't trying to be mean, so Kaede didn't protest much.

"Ah-ha-ha, I'm just messing with you. Anyway, if you've gotten that far, I guess you've got a pretty clear build in mind, huh?"

"Yes! I'm a great shielder, specializing in defense! And... Oh, I suppose I should fill you in."

Kaede proceeded to tell Risa all about her skills and stats.

"Your character is broken as hell, girl! I shoulda known you'd go waaaay off the beaten track, Kaede."

"Er...you think so?"

"Yeah! And you've got the kinda power you can only get if you're way out in left field. It's gonna be hard catching up to you..."

"B-but if you just do what I did...?"

Risa snapped her hands up in an X in front of her, making a buzzing noise.

"You do you," she said, shaking her hands. "I'm not abusing friend privileges to usurp your skills! But I will take the hint on how to find the more out-there skills. I figure that much is allowed."

"So what *are* you gonna do?"

"If you're a tank with crazy-high defense, then I *could* play a mage...but I think that's way too normal to party up with you. I mean, would you really even need me?"

Risa groaned, thinking about it—but then an idea hit her, and a smile played around the edges of her lips.

"Okay! I got it! I'm gonna be an evasion tank!"

"An...evasion tank?"

"Yup! Pull enemy attacks but negate them all by dodging."

"Ohhh! That sounds cool. But aren't I the tank?"

This seemed like a reasonable question to ask. What good was a whole party of tanks?

"With the two of us together, no matter what happens, we'll take no damage! We always emerge unharmed! Doesn't that sound badass?"

Kaede pictured it in her mind for a few moments before nodding vigorously. She was so excited, she was shaking her hands up and down, too.

"I thought that seemed like a great party concept, so I'm going for it!" Risa said.

"Good luck! I'll keep on raising my defense!"

They agreed to play together that evening, and Risa went back to her seat.

"An evasion tank, though," she whispered. "One of the toughest classes to play...but that's what makes it fun!"

Kaede didn't hear a word of this.

Risa was a true gamer.

She nearly always picked the more challenging goal.

If they really were going to be an invincible party that never took damage, Risa would have to learn to dodge every enemy attack.

*   *   *

No matter how many spells came her way.

No matter how fast the combo.

She imagined herself dodging all of that by a hairbreadth and defeating her foes.

"I'm so excited! What could be better?"

Risa couldn't wait for classes to be over.

"Oh! So this is the starter town!"

Risa drank in the sights, thrilled to be here at last. She looked just like Kaede had on her first day.

"Kaede—sorry, Maple. Your gear is so much better than mine; I'm embarrassed to be seen with you."

It was important to use player names in-game.

"Oh, and my name's Sally."

"Sally...Sally. Okay! I won't forget!"

Maple would have to be very careful not to accidentally call her Risa.

She quickly added Sally to her friend list, and they formed a party. Sally showed Maple her stats.

Sally

Lv1   HP 32/32   MP 25/25

[STR 10 ⟨+11⟩]   [VIT 0]
[AGI 55 ⟨+5⟩]   [DEX 25]
[INT 10]

Equipment

Head	[None]	Body	[None]
R. Hand	[Starter Dagger]	L. Hand	[None]
Legs	[None]	Feet	[Starter Magic Boots]
Accessories	[None]		
	[None]		
	[None]		

Skills

None

"You put points in all sorts of stats."

"That's normal! But I'm not sinking anything in VIT, HP, or MP for now."

"Why not?"

"If I dodge everything, who needs Vitality or HP?! And I dunno if I'll be using magic or not, so I'm leaving MP and INT on the low side. STR is enough to let me equip most weapons."

"You really thought this through!"

Maple just put all her points in VIT every time, so there wasn't much to think about.

"Heh-heh-heh...there's a lot more to consider than someone who can soak any blow without taking damage. Wait, didn't you say you got a special prize for coming in third?"

Maple's equipment was exactly what she'd told Sally about before.

"It was just a keepsake medal. I'd been hoping for some decent gear, but..."

"Hmm… Well, maybe the next event will be better. So? Where we going?"

Maple explained why she was headed to the underground lake, and Sally started nodding. Looked like she had a plan.

"Leave it to me! I have an idea."

Maple was all ears.

Sally was running flat out toward the underground lake. Even in a game, too much activity would wear your brain out and you'd slow down, but the rate that happened varied by player.

Reaction speed and stamina depended on how much exertion each player's brain could handle, so they were considered highly variable and mostly based on the player's own gaming ability.

Sally's ability to run like this came from her experience playing a *lot* of VR games.

Meanwhile, Maple…

…was clinging to Sally's back.

She'd removed all her heavy gear, so most casual observers probably wouldn't recognize her.

The Strength stat didn't affect what characters could equip, but carrying a fully geared Maple would have required Sally to have quite a bit of excess STR.

That's why Maple had stashed her gear in her inventory.

"Three wolves up ahead! Maple!" Sally called. Her initial wave of excitement had worn off, and she was all business now, barking clear orders. Maple found it much easier to process things than she had on her own.

"Got it!" Maple called. Sally put her down and backed off.

They were splitting the workload. With her high AGI, Sally was carrying Maple to the lake at a fast clip; meanwhile, Maple

took care of any enemies they encountered on the way. Using this method, they reached the lake in one-fifth the time it had taken Maple solo.

"Wow! That was soooo fast!" Maple said, putting her equipment back on.

Sally was pleased to be useful already.

"Feel free to worship me!" she boasted.

"Ha-ha-ha! All hail Sally!"

That was enough goofing off. They both started fishing. Sally had bought her own fishing rod, so they sat side by side, lines dangling in the water.

An hour after they'd started…

"F-finally! A third fish!"

"Oh, there you go!"

Maple had caught three fish.

Sally was on her twelfth.

"Coming here at level one means I'm racking up the levels just stabbing the fish I hooked!"

Sally was now level 6.

And…

"I got the Fishing skill! What a weird skill to get first. Can't make fun of you now, Maple."

The conditions for getting the Fishing skill required a DEX: 20, so Maple would *never* get it.

"You aren't spending your stat points, Sally?"

"I wanna get a few more skills first. Those'll determine my

combat style, so…I think I'll hold on to my points for now. The beginner stats should be enough to carry me awhile."

"Now you're talking like a hard-core gamer!"

"I'm not *that* bad, but I've certainly played more than you."

They fished for another hour.

Maple's results did not improve.

But with the Fishing skill, Sally caught twenty-four.

"Well? Is that enough?"

"Hmm… I think one more hour should do it."

"No prob! But there's something I wanna try, so…instead of fishing, mind if I dive to catch 'em?"

"Sure, but…can you even do that?"

"I think so! I mean, Maple, you've been trying stuff out without being sure it would work since you started. With my Agility, I should be able to swim through a school of fish and take out at least *one*. I'm good at swimming!"

Sally did a few stretches and promptly hopped into the lake.

"Good luck, then!"

"Thanks! I'll nab as many as I can!"

Sally dived under the water. She swam around for roughly an hour before taking a break. She was a little out of breath but clearly had plenty of stamina—it was easy to forget she'd run the whole way here.

"It became way easier once I got Swimming I and Diving I!"

She took eighty white scales out of her inventory.

"Can I have all of them?"

"Sure, I don't need 'em… But make sure you return the favor someday."

"Will do! Just say the word!"

Maple put the scales in her inventory.

"Maple," Sally said, a gleam in her eye. "You said they'd only found two dungeons?"

"Er...um, that's right."

"I found a small side passage at the bottom of the lake."

"...! That means...!"

Sally nodded, barely able to contain her excitement.

"It *might* be the entrance to a dungeon...but..."

"Oh. I can't come with you."

With Maple's stats, she wouldn't be much use underwater. She'd just rack up her first death drowning.

"So I think I'm gonna carefully clear that. Maybe I'll get myself some unique series gear like you did. But that means..."

Maple nodded, already ahead of her.

"You'll need help getting back to the lake, right? Happy to return the favor!"

"Glad to hear it! I knew I could count on you, Maple!"

"Ha-ha-ha, I aim to please!"

When the day was done, they could just log out, so Sally dived back under, aiming to evolve her Swimming and Diving skills.

CHAPTER 8
Defense Build and Underground Lake Conquest

----

532 Name: Anonymous Great Shielder
Who's been to the second zone? I just made it there myself!

533 Name: Anonymous Spear Master
Same here!
Just cleared that boss earlier

534 Name: Anonymous Greatsworder
I managed it, too

535 Name: Anonymous Mage
Yep
Downed the thing
Woo

536 Name: Anonymous Archer
I made it through somehow

537 Name: Anonymous Spear Master
Huh. We're all pretty good, then?

538 Name: Anonymous Greatsworder
I thought Maple was gonna hit it up first thing, so I was grinding
levels to keep up...

Now I'm a front-runner

539 Name: Anonymous Archer
I did the exact same thing

540 Name: Anonymous Great Shielder
Meanwhile, Maple...
Is still hanging out in the first zone
And from her entry on my friend list, she's formed a party

541 Name: Anonymous Archer
I think I saw 'em

542 Name: Anonymous Mage
Tell us more

543 Name: Anonymous Archer
Dunno her name, but she was in starter gear, clearly friendly, probably real-life buddies.

544 Name: Anonymous Greatsworder
Weapon?

545 Name: Anonymous Archer
Dagger

546 Name: Anonymous Mage
Surprising
I'd have predicted a mage or an archer

547 Name: Anonymous Spear Master
Same

548 Name: Anonymous Great Shielder
Not a bad idea if it's just the two of 'em.
But...she's Maple's friend, right?
She ain't no ordinary beginner.
I'm guessing she's more the Maple type.

549 Name: Anonymous Mage
Highly likely

550 Name: Anonymous Archer
Maple: Extreme builds are superstrong!
Friend: They are?! Then I'll do that!

^ This

551 Name: Anonymous Greatsworder
A party of two Maples
We're all doomed

552 Name: Anonymous Spear Master

Calm down
She's a dagger user

553 Name: Anonymous Mage
Ohhhh
Yeah, in my mind I had her with a great shield, too

554 Name: Anonymous Great Shielder
Dagger user = specializes in AGI?

555 Name: Anonymous Archer
Doesn't seem that good on paper

556 Name: Anonymous Greatsworder
No defense, meaning death anytime she takes a hit
And does no damage

557 Name: Anonymous Spear Master
I'm sure she'll make a name for herself soon.
Maybe the next event?

558 Name: Anonymous Great Shielder
That's a month off. I'm hearing they'll speed time up so it isn't
synced with the real world.
So the event'll last two real hours, but because of the time dilation,
you can't come in late or leave early.
Last time was hype, so management wants to hold them more
often

559 Name: Anonymous Mage
Wise decision

560 Name: Anonymous Spear Master
A month should get her ready
Figure out her play style
We'll know then

561 Name: Anonymous Greatsworder
This event needs to be tomorrow
I gotta see what this girl is like

Unaware that they were being talked about…

Maple and Sally were at the underground lake again, fishing and swimming. Well, Maple sometimes went outside, lay down, and—for some reason—used Taunt to make monsters attack her.

She'd been planning on grinding damage-reduction skills after getting a new shield made, so right now she was actually trying to find undiscovered skills. It wasn't really going well, but Maple was still having fun trying.

It had already been two weeks since Sally started playing.

They weren't necessarily always coordinating schedules and logging in together.

Sally simply played whenever she could find time, grabbing a wide range of easily acquired skills (beyond just Swimming and Diving).

They were both prepping for the next event while spending a lot of time at the lake so Sally could clear the dungeon she'd found down there.

"*Gasp…!* Haah…haah…how long was I under?" Sally said, surfacing.

"W-wow! That was forty minutes!" Maple said.

"With Swimming X and Diving X, that's my current max... twenty minutes each way, so if I don't turn back in time, I'll drown."

"Want me to send you a friend message at the twenty-minute mark? You should hear a ding when that happens, so you'll know."

"Great idea, Maple! Yeah, let's do that."

"Got it! Enjoy your dive!"

"Here goes nothing!"

Sally swam toward the bottom at incredible speed.

Deeper and deeper, through clear water and schools of white fish. She could soon see waterweeds swaying and rocks studding the floor. Between two of these rocks was a gap in the lake wall, and Sally slipped inside. The interior was lit by a bluish glow cast by some aquatic plants.

Just as she'd suspected, the cave continued for quite a while, leading farther and farther down. She swam on, fast as any fish.

When she arrived at a branch, Sally stopped. She'd been assuming it would be a single channel all the way through.

Grumbling about the lost time, she began exploring right and left, mentally mapping the place.

A while later, she got a message from Maple. Twenty minutes down.

There were no monsters in this passage, so there were no unexpected delays; she made it back to Maple safely.

"Haah...haah..."

Sally pulled herself up on land, trying to catch her breath.

"Well?"

"There's a lot of forks along the way. I'm gonna give it one more shot today. No idea how deep it goes."

"Okay, I'll ping you again."

Sally dived back in. She knew her way through the first part of the maze now, so she took the quickest path…

…and started marking off one dead end after another, moving deeper and deeper.

Just as she got another alert from Maple…

…Sally found her path blocked by a large white door.

She pumped her fist in victory and turned back. Sally wasn't about to blow her shot at a unique series, so she intended to make sure she was thoroughly prepared.

"Boss room! Found it…haah…haah…"

She reached up from the water and gave Maple a high five. Now she just had to beat the thing.

"I'm gonna rest a minute and then head in! No time like the present. You?"

"I think I'm gonna log out."

"Cool. Thanks for tagging along."

"No prob!"

Maple vanished in a cloud of light.

Sally took a moment to focus.

"What about my stats…?"

Sally

Lv12   HP 32/32   MP 25/25   ⟨+10⟩

[STR 10 ⟨+11⟩]   [VIT 0]
[AGI 55 ⟨+5⟩]   [DEX 25]
[INT 10]

Equipment

Head	[None]	Body	[None]
R. Hand	[Starter Dagger]	L. Hand	[None]
Legs	[None]	Feet	[Starter Magic Boots]
Accessories	[None]		
	[None]		
	[None]		

Skills

Slash, Double Slash, Gale Slash

Down Attack, Power Attack, Switch Attack

Fire Ball, Water Ball, Wind Cutter

Sand Cutter, Dark Ball

Refresh

Affliction II

Strength Boost (S), Combo Boost (S), Martial Arts I

MP Boost (S), MP Cost Down (S), MP Recovery Speed
Boost (S), Poison Resist (S)

Gathering Speed Boost (S)

Dagger Mastery II, Magic Mastery II

Fire Magic I, Water Magic I, Wind Magic I

Earth Magic I, Dark Magic I, Light Magic I

Presence Block II, Presence Detect II, Sneaky Steps I,
Leap I

Fishing, Swimming X, Diving X, Cooking I

"I've got thirty-five stat points, but I think I'll hold off on distributing them for now. I wanna win by dodging."

She had a *lot* more skills than Maple did—she'd been sacrificing her sleep time to unlock them all.

Her MP cost was reduced by 7 percent.
And the recovery speed increased by 5 percent. She also had a straight boost of +10 MP.

Her STR was increased by 5 percent.
During combos, she got a buff to STR that could go as high as 10 percent.

"Right! Let's do this!"
Her strategy set, Sally made her way back to the white doors.

The doors slowly swung open. The room inside was a giant sphere, half-filled with water.
Having oxygen available was a pleasant surprise. This meant she didn't have to force the battle to a quick conclusion.

"*Gasp!* ...Okay...come at me!"
Sally's eyes had a glint of steel. As if to answer the call, the light coalesced, taking shape—and a giant white fish appeared.
The massive fish shot forward, its enormous bulk hurtling toward her.
Sally read the attack perfectly, twisting her frame, narrowly avoiding it and slashing its scales as it passed, her dagger glowing red.

"Slash!"
The poisonous purple hue beneath the red glow was proof Affliction II had kicked in.
Her strike applied a poison effect.

It didn't do *that* much, but the giant fish's HP was slowly drained away.

It swung around and came charging at her again.

Once more, Sally evaded the charge and hit it in passing.

"Wind Cutter!"

Red damage effects gleamed beneath the water. Sally's strongest spell had left shallow cuts along the fish's scales.

The fish kept charging, but it was unable to harm her.

She had its health down to 80 percent now.

She focused, watching it carefully.

Most players wouldn't see the difference, but to Sally's eyes, this charge was totally different. It was subtly—but noticeably—slower.

The giant fish stopped mid-charge, swinging its tail—a wide-ranging attack aimed forward.

But even this failed to reach Sally.

She'd been using the boss's HP bar as a rough guide to when it would change up its attack pattern.

Correctly estimating the range of its attack from its size, she'd moved one step outside, waiting for the tail to swing past. Then she used a skill to slice the tail.

"Double Slash!"

Sally had kept her combo going without taking damage, so she was now at the maximum damage boost.

Two red effects slashed the fish's tail, gouging just a bit deeper than before.

And as they did, Affliction II injected a paralytic, slowing the boss's movements.

"Power Attack!"

Her dagger buried itself in the sluggish fish's side—to the hilt. Sally quickly yanked it out, moving backward. The boss's HP dropped below 50 percent.

Time for a new attack phase.

White magic circles appeared on both sides of the fish, spewing bubbles.

"Water Ball!"

Sally's spell hit the bubbles, and there was a thunderous explosion. Sally was certain she could not afford to touch those bubbles directly.

She fled the fish, sending spells ahead of her to clear the bubbles and open a path.

The fish's attack pattern had switched to pursuit, chasing after her. Sally was well aware of this.

And she knew just what to do.

She spun round, detonating the bubbles with a water spell. A momentary gap opened up, and she corkscrewed herself through it.

"Power Attack!"

A red effect traced a single line down the fish's back.

A deep gouge from head to tail that knocked its HP all the way to just above 20 percent. And as she reached the tail, Sally turned once more and took several swipes at the fins.

It turned to follow her again, but the bubbles couldn't keep up—and for a moment, the bubble barrier thinned.

Sally seized her chance.

"Wind Cutter!"

Her wind blades shot between the bubbles, cutting deep. Its HP was now below 20 percent, and the bar turned red.

As it did, the magic circles flanking the fish vanished, and the room filled with water.

The walls above, below, and on all sides were now covered in magic circles, all of them generating bubbles.

The giant fish's maw opened wide. A magic circle appeared inside, glowing with a powerful light, far brighter than the bubble generators.

Years of gaming had honed Sally's instincts, and she moved on reflex alone.

A moment later, a high-velocity water beam ripped through the space she'd just vacated.

Sally gulped. It would take a lot of luck to dodge that twice.

And the bubbles were closing in.

This was bad—so bad, she was losing her cool.

Panic made it hard to think straight.

Moments like this required a calm mind.

Sally told herself this. Focusing, trying to settle herself down.

It was as if time had stopped.

The bubbles, the beam, even the giant fish's movements.

Sally took note of them, every last one, like they were in slow motion.

She knew exactly where she was safe and where she would be in danger.

Every twitch of her foe, every glance—they were all cues that told her where the beam would go next.

The current position of the bubbles told her where they'd mess her up, so she swam ahead, making escape routes. Building on past experiences, aggressively increasing her odds of survival.

It was downright prophetic.

There were hacks less powerful than her raw gaming ability.

"Wind Cutter," she said softly.

The spell slipped through the gaps in the bubbly curtain, gouging the fish.

And at last…

…the boss's HP bar was empty.

◆□◆□◆□◆□◆

All the water in the room drained away, and a giant treasure chest appeared in the center.

Sally flopped down on her back, too tired to celebrate.

"Argh...concentrating like that really takes it out of you..."

Alerts for new skills and levels played, but she stayed put, figuring she could check them later.

She'd been hoping to avoid needing to concentrate that much, but between the wall of exploding bubbles and the laser cannon, it hadn't left her much choice.

After a long rest, Sally recovered enough to scope out the chest.

"Open sesame!" she yelled, flinging it open with both hands.

Inside was a scarf, blue as the sea but white at the ends, like bubbles. A knee-length blue coat and an outfit to match.

And two daggers, of a blue as dark as the depths of the ocean, beyond light's reach. Scabbards for the daggers and a blue belt.

Sally went through each piece, scoping them out.

Surface Scarf

[AGI +10] [MP +10] [Indestructible]
Skill: Mirage

Oceanic Coat

[AGI +30] [MP +15] [Indestructible]
Skill: Oceanic

Oceanic Clothes

[AGI +20] [MP +10] [Indestructible]

Deep Sea Dagger

[STR +20] [DEX +10] [Indestructible]

Seabed Dagger

[INT +20] [DEX +10] [Indestructible]

"Huh…are these generated based on my skill spread? Heh-heh. Definitely my style. More pieces than Maple's gear, but these don't have any skill slots or the Destructive Growth trait."

She equipped all her new gear and did a little spin out of sheer happiness. The belt seemed to count as part of the shorts and didn't take up an equipment slot.

Like Maple, Sally was now wearing a unique series outfit that provided major stat boosts—but, unlike Maple's, to a number of different stats.

She left the cave, deciding she and Maple could figure out the next skills they were going after tomorrow. She was too tired to do it now.

The next day…

"Wow! You look so good!"

"I know, right? I didn't get any footwear, so I bought some black boots—but everything matches!"

Together, they went through her new skills.

First, the skills her new gear provided.

After that, the skills she'd acquired during the fight—one of which Maple already knew.

Mirage

On activation, creates a discrepancy between target's location and opponent's visual feedback.
Affects everyone but user.
Use limit is ten times per day.
Effect lasts five seconds.
Effect lost if the false image created by Mirage is attacked.

Oceanic

Emits a horizonal circle of water centered on user that reduces monster/player AGI by 20% on contact. Cannot be used in the air.
Fixed radius of ten yards.
Only the user is immune.
Use limit is three times per day. Effect lasts ten seconds.

Jack of All Trades

−30% damage dealt. −10% MP cost.
[AGI +10] [DEX +10]

Condition

Ten weapon/attack skills acquired.
Ten magic/MP skills acquired.
Ten other skills acquired.
Ten or more of these skills are at the lowest level.
Defeat a monster with these conditions met.

*   *   *

And the last skill was Giant Killing.

"Ohhh…interesting, interesting. If I'd picked up Jack of All Trades before that fight, I would have been screwed."

She thought about it awhile.

"I don't really need Giant Killing…"

"Huh? Why not?"

"I mean, it's real good for *you*, Maple. But since I'm not putting all my points into one thing, having my AGI go up and down would mess with my senses."

Having her stats change without her realizing it could disrupt the timing of her dodges, so it was a poor fit for Sally's play style.

"I see…"

"Guess I should scrap it…"

"What's that?"

"Huh?"

"Huh?"

They blinked at each other.

"I had no idea you could scrap skills!"

"I'm…surprised that's even possible! But if you do scrap a skill, the only way to get it back is if you go to a specific location and pay five hundred thousand G, so only do it if you *really* don't want the skill."

And with that, Sally scrapped Giant Killing.

She was now level 15.

She had forty stat points saved up but still wasn't spending any.

"That should do it! Oh, right, Maple, what's up with your gear?"

"Well, for now I'm just having her make the great shield. That's the most important piece. I can get a matching short sword and armor later."

Iz was already working on the shield.

"Cool! We've got that event coming up… Can't hurt to gather a few more skills."

"Then…you wanna head to the second zone? Oh, but is that best? I mean, they probably have unique series there, too. Would you rather solo the zone dungeon?"

Since the condition for reaching the second zone required you to clear a dungeon, doing that solo would likely net them some really good gear.

"Hmm… I don't think so. I like this gear."

"If you're fine, I'm fine. Let's run this dungeon together!"

"Great! Let's head on over!"

They made their way to the zone entrance dungeon, using the same traversal technique they'd used to get to the underground lake.

"This is so faaast!"

"Hang on tight!"

Their next destination was in the north.

At this speed, it would not take long to get there.

CHAPTER 9

Defense Build and Second Zone Conquest

"We're here!"

"All right! Let's get in there!"

The entrance to the ruins was made of stone.

If their information was correct, the dungeon here led to the second zone.

Maple took the lead. Holding Night's Facsimile as she walked, she was ready for anything.

Not long after, they encountered a monster.

First up was a rather large boar. It had massive tusks, and both girls thought it must have pretty high DPS.

"Wind Cutter!"

Sally started the fight with a spell. But it carved only 20 percent off the boar's life.

"Hngg… My damage really did take a nasty hit. I'll have to up my Affliction skill to compensate."

But while she was muttering, the boar had righted itself and charged in. It was moments away from slamming into Maple when…

...the shield swallowed it.

"Uh...mind if I leave the boar fights to you?"

"No prob!"

It was a narrow path, so every time a boar charged, it killed itself.

But the boars didn't know about Maple's shield, so they just kept charging.

Each time the path branched, they explored the side passages, slowly making their way to the back.

"Oh! A new enemy!" Maple said.

A bear had appeared from around the bend.

Maple raised her shield in case it came charging in, but no such luck.

The bear waved one massive paw, and a white claw-shaped effect shot toward them.

It hit Maple's shield and was swallowed instantly, but it was more than enough to surprise her.

"Th-that's new!" she said.

"Didn't think bears would be long-range attackers! It's keeping its distance but blocking our progress."

This bear had much better AI than the boars, so it must be higher level.

Sally put a hand to her mouth, thinking.

"I'll handle this one," she said. "You just keep your shield held in front."

Sally whispered something under her breath. To Maple's eyes, it looked like the shield fell from her hands.

The bear seemed to see the same thing and seized its chance, rushing forward.

If Maple hadn't clearly felt the shield still in her hands, she'd have ducked down to pick it up.

The bear reached her invisible shield...and vanished.

The empty space warped, revealing her great shield again. The fake on the ground disappeared.

"Guess my Mirage experiment worked!"

"Mirage?! I saw my shield fall and was so confused!"

"I wanted to try that out once, but there is a use limit, so I'll save the rest for the boss. I'll leave most of the fighting to you."

"Okay! I can handle it!"

Maple and Sally headed farther in. It wasn't that long a dungeon, and they only fought ten more monsters before reaching the boss room.

They opened the huge doors and went inside.

The room beyond had a high ceiling and was quite long. At the very back was an enormous tree.

As they stepped in, the doors closed behind them.

And…

The tree started cracking, shifting, and transforming—into a giant deer.

The antlers on the deer's head were covered in green leaves, and bright red apples hung from the branches.

The boss shook its wooden body, stamped the earth, and glared at the two girls.

"Here it comes!"

"Okay!"

Green magic circles appeared at the deer's feet.

This signaled the start of the battle.

The deer stomped the ground, and the circles flashed. One massive vine after another broke from the ground, shooting toward the girls.

"Whoa!"

"Ha-ha! Too slow!"

The vines hit Maple's shield head-on and were immediately swallowed up. Sally, meanwhile, used her patented evasive maneuvers to dodge the coiling onslaught.

Maple's New Moon was their main damage dealer.

She unleashed a dragon made of poison, as if to counter the vines.

It swallowed up those tendrils, melting them, and threatened the deer itself.

But before it struck home, a glittering green barrier blocked it, and the dragon vanished.

"Huh??"

"It's those magic circles, I think! Our attacks won't reach! There's gotta be a gimmick somewhere!"

The deer was sending more vines forth. This wasn't a problem for either of them, fortunately.

They endured for a few minutes but weren't getting anywhere.

"I'm gonna go all out on a scouting run. Can you tank for a bit?"

"Sure! Taunt!"

All the vines turned toward Maple. Sally raced off to try a few things.

She threw out a bunch of spells, causing the barrier to manifest—and then noticed something interesting.

"You can attack the antlers! And it looks like those apples might be maintaining the barrier!"

She pointed up at the dangling fruit. The apples shone red each time the barrier appeared—tiny magic circles spinning around them.

"Okay! Leave it to me! I'll blow them all away!"

"Cool, go for it."

Maple thrust New Moon out in front of her. Sally had said their attacks could hit the antlers, so she knew right where to aim. No barrier appeared to block the poison dragon—and it swallowed up the wooden antlers, melting them and annihilating the apples.

"Wind Cutter!"

Sally went on the offensive immediately. This time the barrier did not interfere, and her attack reached the deer. Sally had been right; the apples were part of its defenses. Red visual damage effects sprouted all across the deer.

"Great! It worked!"

"Pulling out a big move!"

The crystals on Maple's shield started snapping, and a massive purple circle deployed around New Moon. The light of it grew steadily, forming a three-headed poison dragon—which lunged at the deer.

The deer's body melted, spraying red effects in all directions. This was clearly critical damage.

But the green magic circles at the deer's feet glowed again, healing its wounds. Its HP bar recovered to 20 percent, and the poison status effect was cleared. With that, the circles' effect ended, and they faded away.

"Can you hit it again?"

"I can, but it'll take time!"

But the deer wasn't waiting for them to chat it out. It changed up its attack patterns, launching wind blades and ever more massive vines their way.

And...

"!"

"Whoaaaaaaaaaaaa!"

The ground beneath their feet suddenly rose up, attacking. Sally sensed it in time and dodged, but Maple was flung into the air.

She didn't take any damage, but she was slammed into the ground—which gave her the stun status effect and left her immobilized. Normally that would make survival improbable, but seeing as how wind blades were hitting her and her HP bar wasn't going down at all, she would clearly have no issues surviving until she woke up.

But this meant it would take that much longer for Maple's skill to activate.

"Well, fine. Didn't really wanna, but…"

Sally hefted a dagger in each hand and broke into a run.

Despite her grumbling, there was a grin on her face.

"Guess I'll just have to kill ya."

She saw every attack coming.

When Sally was this focused, it was like the attacks didn't even exist. She slipped through the gaps between them, right to the deer's feet, and then used Leap I to propel herself into the air before its very eyes.

The one spot on the battlefield safe from its wind blades.

"Did you notice you'd left a gap here? Double Slash!"

Her body spun, and the twin daggers in her hands flashed, landing four strikes in all.

Wielding two weapons doubled the number of attacks, and while each slash did less overall damage, the quantity compensated for the difference.

Then Sally ran up the deer's face and onto its back.

"Power Attack!"

Two long gashes were opened from its brow to its tail.

Then a fire spell set its back ablaze.

As Sally flitted around it, wind blades flew at her...

But she dodged them easily.

"Mm? This wasn't a safe zone, then?"

She was slipping between wind blades as if she was threading a needle, attacking every chance she got, slowly chipping away at the deer's HP bar.

"Hngg... O-oh! Right! We're in a fight!"

Maple finally got up and fixed her eyes on the deer...

Just in time to watch it explode in a shower of light particles.

"Whaaaaaat?!"

"Finished it off while you were napping," Sally said, landing near her.

For Maple, their dungeon conquest had ended on a rather unsatisfying note.

Be that as it may, the two of them had earned the right to advance to the second zone.

CHAPTER 10

Defense Build and Maintenance

"Awww…"

Maple and Sally had started basing their activities around the second zone's town, but Maple was looking rather gloomy.

"Hngg… First, they go into maintenance mode two weeks before the event. And then, worst of all…"

They'd both logged in the moment maintenance ended, but when they saw the results, they'd received quite a shock.

Well, mostly Maple.

The maintenance had rolled out a patch, adjusting skill effects and conditions, while also improving field monster AI.

The names of skills affected weren't made public, so only people who actually had the skills knew what had changed.

And there was one more big change.

Specifically…

They'd added skills that penetrated defense and reduced pain accordingly.

There were three to five of these per weapon type, and they were solidly powerful.

These skills reduced the overall pain levels attacks dished out to compensate for this…but it was the skill adjustments that really hurt Maple.

"Awww…"

"Well, this happens when you get too much attention. Your approach made certain builds way stronger than the devs intended."

Sally was patting her shoulders.

Maple had received two key nerfs.

But given what Sally had just said, perhaps it was really three.

First, the patch had gone after Devour.

The adjustments had added a limit of ten uses a day but doubled the MP it absorbed.

Since it was essentially always active, once her shield got hit ten times, Night's Facsimile would turn into a perfectly ordinary great shield. Since it now absorbed twice as much MP, it did still serve as a decent MP tank, but it was clearly a significant nerf.

Next, the AI improvements made monsters more likely to run around and attack from behind or even run away entirely.

Sally had told Maple this was largely to prevent anyone else turning out like her. Maple didn't seem to get what that meant, so Sally gave her the long version.

"I mean, if the AI is better, then nobody can use the white rabbits to shortcut their way to your core skill, Absolute Defense. The improved AI means the rabbits won't attack you for an hour straight—I think it's safe to assume management didn't expect anyone to get it that way."

The maintenance would prevent the reoccurrence of an irregular like Maple, but Sally also promised they weren't doing the maintenance *just* to target Maple and wouldn't go so far as to kill her build outright.

"Like, they can't remove Absolute Defense entirely. I bet many top players had their stronger skills nerfed a bit. And your Devour just happened to be one of them."

"Hmm… Well, I guess that's okay. It was pretty overpowered. But the last thing…"

"That means you'll actually be taking damage now. That change was definitely targeting you. It's a bit roundabout, but…skills like that exist in a *lot* of games."

"Hnggggg…"

Maple's durability was so obviously off the charts that management had been forced to resort to desperate measures and made some wide-reaching adjustments.

"Piercing skills are pretty standard, and frankly, you've had it a bit too easy," Sally said.

Maple put her hands together, looking apologetic.

"Oh…sorry," she said. "I'm not invincible anymore! Now our party won't be, either! Even though you stepped up to be our evasion tank."

They'd set out to form a party that would, ideally, never take damage. But that was no longer possible.

"Not your fault! And sure, you *can* take damage now, but…that just means you aren't *always* invincible. Besides, if you can find a way to make it so you've got damage effects going all over the place and they keep chipping away at you, but you—Just! Won't! Die!—then that'll make you seem even *more* invincible. And then...you smile. Wouldn't that be megacool?"

Maple pictured herself chuckling as the enemy desperately rained blows down on her, clinging to the hope that they were doing *some* damage, only for her to turn the tables once they'd worn themselves out.

"Oh...I do like the sound of that..."

"You just let out a *very* sinister chuckle."

"Wh-whoa! I didn't mean it! I take it back!" Maple yelped, waving her hands frantically.

Sally laughed it off. "Hmm...but I guess this means you'll have to boost your HP somehow. Can't have the pierce damage shredding you. Can you handle the pain?"

"Well...if I have to, I guess? It's not as bad as the real world. And it seems like they've reduced the pain levels."

"So you need to knuckle down and block as much as possible... then get your hands on some recovery skills and equipment, maybe some that boost HP and MP?"

With that, she'd end up being basically invincible, or so Sally said.

"I'll help you gather the equipment! And look for any skills that might help."

"Y-you're sure?"

"I got you into this game! I have no problem doing all that if it'll help us enjoy it together. Wanna go now?"

"Sure! Thanks!"

"I'll probably want your help eventually, too."

"Of course! I'll do whatever I can when the time comes!"

Maple was all smiles now.

"Right, then… First, let's get a few skills that raise your HP. That seems like the priority. I know some already, and the event's coming up, so we'd better hurry!"

"Yeah!"

They ran off across the field.

To get new skills, to cover Maple's weaknesses, and to post good results in the event together.

They just had to focus on what they could do right now.

On the second day of their grinding…

Maple was in the second zone town, thinking about the best uses for Devour.

She couldn't use it willy-nilly like she had been, so she'd have to be stingier with it and carefully choose her opportunities.

"Um…so I definitely need to raise my defense even more, making it harder to take damage…"

All she could really do was keep boosting her VIT value until she didn't even *need* a shield to block blows.

"Maybe with a few more levels…"

Maple got to her feet, but before she could head out to the field, she received a message.

"Mm? Oh! It's from Iz!"

Maple read the message and discovered her new shield was ready.

"Right! That'll help me switch up my tactics!"

Maple had *just* been thinking about Devour conservation, so this message had arrived with flawless timing.

"I'd better go pick it up!"

Maple made a beeline for Iz's shop.

Upon her arrival, she wasted no time heading inside.

Iz was behind the counter. Their eyes met.

"Oh, Maple! That was quick."

"It's really ready?!"

"Of course! Here you go."

Maple took the pure-white great shield—named White Snow—and equipped it.

It was beautifully decorated, white as freshly fallen snow, but with blue gems embedded here and there on the surface. It was every bit as impressive-looking as Night's Facsimile.

"Thank you so much!" Maple said, gazing at it with evident delight.

Iz grinned back. "It looks good on you! It should be pretty durable, but make sure to bring it in for maintenance regularly. It would suck if it broke."

"Okay!" Maple said enthusiastically.

"And…try fighting with it once. I did my best to match the size, but if you're struggling with it, I can always adjust it."

"Got it. Thanks again!"

They chatted a bit more, and then Maple put White Snow in her inventory and left the shop.

Outside, Maple went straight into the field.

Like Iz suggested, she wanted to try White Snow out.

"Um, then…I suppose I should do the training Sally recommended while I'm at it!"

Two birds with one shield. Maple was all fired up.

*   *   *

She and Sally had been gathering skills for a week now—one more week till the event started.

Once again, Maple was on her own, looking for new skills.

"I never realized until Sally told me, but I don't have *any* of the skills great shielders usually use in parties."

Sally had told her the core great-shield skills had a wealth of defense and Vitality benefits, so whenever she got a chance, she was out here on her own, trying to master the basics.

She and Sally had already worked together, getting a number of HP-boosting and MP-boosting skills.

Maple checked her current stats, wondering what she needed next.

Maple

Lv24	HP 40/40 ⟨+60⟩	MP 12/12 ⟨+10⟩

[STR 0]   [VIT 170 ⟨+66⟩]
[AGI 0]   [DEX 0]
[INT 0]

Equipment

Head	[None]	Body	[Black Rose Armor]
R. Hand	[New Moon: Hydra]	L. Hand	[Night's Facsimile: Devour]
Legs	[Black Rose Armor]	Feet	[Black Rose Armor]
Accessories	[Forest Queen Bee Ring]		
	[Toughness Ring]		
	[None]		

Skills

Shield Attack, Sidestep, Deflect, Meditation, Taunt
HP Boost (S), MP Boost (S)
Great Shield Mastery IV
Absolute Defense, Moral Turpitude, Giant Killing, Hydra
Eater, Bomb Eater

Getting HP Boost (S) and MP Boost (S) had given her an extra thirty HP and an extra ten MP.

Then Sally had given her the Toughness Ring, which granted another thirty HP.

That didn't feel like much, but it was more than double what Maple had started with.

Sally had said she was going to acquire a Pierce Attack skill before the event began.

This was specifically so she could get an idea of what sort of damage Maple would be in for. They didn't want to find out mid-event.

"She's done so much for me... I've got to find myself some useful skills."

Maple's eyes paused on one skill in particular.

"Cover Move I and Cover...basic great-shield skills. That I don't have."

Both were skills that protected party members and were only for great shielders. Anyone in a party with a great shield had to have them.

Maple had looked at them before but hadn't needed them then—but now she was in a party, so they were a lot more interesting.

Cover Move I

Move to the location of a party member within a five-yard radius, ignoring AGI.
After use, take 2x damage for thirty seconds.
Use limit is ten.
Use limit recovers every hour.

Condition

Purchase at the Skill Shop.

Cover

Protect nearby party members from damage.
On activation, increase VIT by 10%.

Condition

Purchase at the Skill Shop.

The Skill Shop was run by an NPC and sold basic skills for each type of equipment.

In addition to Cover Move I and Cover, it sold Slash, Double Slash, and so on.

Maple had sold the extra white scales she'd collected at the lake and received a lot of G, so she could easily afford a couple of skills.

"Guess I'm going shopping!"

Maple set out for the NPC shop.

She figured this would allow her to save Sally if she was ever in trouble.

Maple bought both skills and left the shop, carrying a bag with two scrolls—the skills were written on these.

She sat down on a nearby bench and pulled one out of the bag.

When she unrolled it, the letters lit up—and when that light faded, the scroll crumbled, turning to light and fading away.

"Skill: Cover Move I acquired."

"Oh, how pretty!"

Maple took out the Cover scroll and unrolled that, too.

Once again, it lit up and then crumbled into light.

"Oh…it's over already? Were there any other skills I needed?"

There weren't. She had checked ahead of time to see what skills she needed.

"Oh well! Maybe they'll add more someday. Guess I'll do what Sally said and work on my own gaming ability!"

She enthusiastically headed back to the second zone field.

"Ugh…I'm so slow. Too slow. Was I always this slow?"

Maple was in a desert Sally had told her about. She'd made her way out into it and then stopped. According to Sally, this was currently the best place for Maple's goals.

"Hmm… I don't see any enemies… Yikes!"

A sudden blow from behind almost knocked her off her feet.

Naturally, she took no damage, so her life wasn't in danger.

"Wh-what the...? Oh, is that—?"

A monster that resembled a pill bug was rolling around behind her. That must be what had tackled her.

It rolled around for a while, then uncurled and began burrowing under the sand.

"I get it! That's how I practice defense!"

Maple took out the white shield that Iz had made for her.

White Snow

[VIT +40]

Unlike Night's Facsimile, it had a simple description, no skills at all—but at the moment, the VIT boost was actually stronger.

This probably proved just how good Iz was. She was the best crafter around, capable of supplying the top players in the game.

"Okay, let's get to work!"

Maple hefted her shield, and a pill bug bounced off the back of her head.

"Eep! G-gimme a second!"

But the monsters were disinclined to do so. As she was midscream, they hit her again.

"Ugh...n-now I'm mad!"

She scrambled to her feet, hefted her shield, and perked up her ears.

According to Sally, it was important to determine the location of enemies from the sounds of their movement. Following her instructions, Maple was focused on that, doing her best to detect her enemies' locations.

"Hmm...here!"

Maple held her shield up to her right. A pill bug was charging in, and it bounced off the shield, falling backward.

"Great...aiiiieee!"

Maple was so pleased she'd detected it that she didn't notice the second pill bug attacking from behind.

"R-right...there's more than one. That makes it harder..."

She spent another two hours fighting them. But by the end, she could block around 40 percent.

Sally said that if she could block all the attacks, then she wouldn't have to worry much about Pierce Attacks no matter where they were.

"But at only forty percent... Well, I worked hard enough for today. How does Sally dodge like that, seriously?"

To Maple's eyes, it looked less like Sally was dodging and more like the attacks were dodging her. With that thought, she logged out for the day.

◆□◆□◆□◆□◆

A little earlier that same day, Sally had just logged in herself. She was thinking about her build.

"Time I spent these points. I'm pretty set on this direction, after all. I want to keep my attack options varied, so...let's go with fifteen to STR, twenty to AGI, and the rest to INT. There go all fifty!"

Sally

Lv18   HP 32/32   MP 25/25 ⟨+35⟩

[STR 25 ⟨+20⟩]   [VIT 0]
[AGI 75 ⟨+68⟩]   [DEX 25 ⟨+20⟩]
[INT 25 ⟨+20⟩]

Equipment

Head	[Surface Scarf: Mirage]	Body	[Oceanic Coat: Oceanic]
R. Hand	[Deep Sea Dagger]	L. Hand	[Seabed Dagger]
Legs	[Oceanic Clothes]	Feet	[Black Boots]
Accessories	[None]		
	[None]		
	[None]		

Skills

Slash, Double Slash, Gale Slash, Defense Break
Down Attack, Power Attack, Switch Attack
Fire Ball, Water Ball, Wind Cutter
Sand Cutter, Dark Ball
Water Wall, Wind Wall, Refresh, Heal
Affliction III
Strength Boost (S), Combo Boost (S), Martial Arts I
MP Boost (S), MP Cost Down (S), MP Recovery Speed
Boost (S), Poison Resist (S)
Gathering Speed Boost (S)

Dagger Mastery II, Magic Mastery II
Fire Magic I, Water Magic II, Wind Magic II
Earth Magic I, Dark Magic I, Light Magic II
Presence Block II, Presence Detect II, Sneaky Steps I,
Leap I
Fishing, Swimming X, Diving X, Cooking I, Jack of All
Trades

"Getting Light Magic to II lets me use Heal…and with Affliction at III, I can inflict more status effects. And I've got a Pierce Attack skill, so I'm good on attacks and support."

Sally closed her status menu and headed to the field. Her destination was in the depths of a forest.

"I wanna get a badass skill while Maple isn't looking. Can't wait to see the look on her face!"

Sally was currently seeking out one of a number of quests available from NPCs.

There was a little house in the depths of the woods, and if you cleared this quest, you could unlock the Superspeed skill.

"AGI: 70 is a prereq, but I got there just in time!"

Like Maple, Sally was getting as strong as she could before the event started.

"Okay, I'm here!"

Sally found herself by a little house in the woods. Nothing particularly remarkable about it—your standard-issue log house.

There was a burbling brook running beside it and a waterwheel turning slowly.

A small field out front and signs that someone had been chopping wood. A number of logs lying ready to chop.

The pleasant sound of birdsong filled Sally's ears.

She approached the house, knocked on the door, and waited.

After a moment, the door swung open.

An elderly man with a long white beard emerged, walking with the aid of a cane.

"Not often we get visitors out here," he said. "Come on in; sit a spell. There's a lot of fearsome monsters in these parts."

He waved Sally through the door. She accepted his generosity.

If you arrived without enough AGI, the man wouldn't answer the door, and nothing would happen at all.

The interior was pretty barren. Just the bare-minimum furniture.

The one thing that drew the eye was the dagger displayed atop a shelf to one side—it was old but clearly an impressive piece.

The old man waved her to a chair by the table, and Sally took a seat.

He put a mug of tea in front of her.

"Drink up! It'll help you relax."

"Uh, thanks. Don't mind if I do."

Sally drank the tea. Like he'd said, she could feel it working.

Specifically, it fully restored her MP.

She hadn't lost any HP, so she couldn't tell, but her intel said it restored that, too.

"Hmph. Feel free to take a load off. I'll go fetch some Magic Water."

Magic Water was, as the name suggested, magic-restoring

water found in a natural spring. NPCs in the second zone town would tell you where it was.

It was pretty far—a good thirty minutes from here.

Sally had been waiting for this moment.

"Oh, I'd be happy to fetch some for you."

"Mm? Would you? I sure would appreciate it. My knees aren't what they used to be."

He gave Sally a glass bottle.

A blue screen appeared in front of Sally.

It had the words YES and NO on it.

Naturally, Sally tapped YES and accepted the quest.

Crafter players had checked out the Magic Water spring right after the second zone opened, but nobody could figure out how to collect the water.

You could drink it right there and recover your MP, but taking it with you was seemingly impossible.

The only way to collect the Magic Water was by using the glass bottle received from this quest.

But it would vanish from your inventory an hour after filling it.

In other words, the spring mostly existed for the sake of this quest.

"I'll be right back!"

"Thanks… I appreciate it."

Sally flew out of the log house, racing toward the spring.

There were three types of monsters in the area.

The first were Big Spiders.

These were arachnids that were over three feet wide. They used their thread to bind their foes, which could be a real pain. This type of attack was Sally's nemesis.

The second enemy was the Sleep Beetle.

These were rhinoceros beetles that inflicted the sleep status effect on their foes. They were slightly larger than real-world beetles but still easy to overlook and quite scary if they caught you off guard.

The third enemy was the treant.

Disguised as trees, they waited to ambush unsuspecting travelers.

But they were the only tree in this forest with red fruit.

Knowing that in advance would make them easier to avoid. Even then, their branches and roots could reach pretty far, and many a player had found their escape routes cut off.

Sally was racing through the woods.

She'd done her homework but encountered no monsters as she ran.

With no serious obstacles getting in the way, it took her exactly thirty minutes to reach the spring.

"Isn't that lovely!" she said.

The clearest water she'd ever seen caught the light, and the sparkles illuminated the trees and plants all around.

It was a magical sight, and Sally stopped to soak it in.

Then she drank a gulp from it, restoring her MP—and focused her mind.

"Here's where it gets tough."

Sally filled the glass bottle and placed it in her inventory. Her time limit: one hour.

If she failed to make it back to the log house in time, it would vanish, and she'd fail the quest.

There'd been no monsters on her way here, but on the way back, the forest would be jam-packed with them.

"Here goes nothing…"

Sally swung around and plunged back into the woods, the shrill screeches of spiders echoing all around.

This was the meat of the quest.

With no monsters, it took half an hour. But with monsters, getting back in just an hour was a real challenge.

The only way to get Superspeed was to overcome this trial.

Spider thread was shooting out of the underbrush and from trees above, whistling past her ears. If any of those hit, she'd be captured...and done for.

"Whoa! ...! Mirage!"

As Sally raced on, a swarm of Sleep Beetles struck her...

And her body warped, dissolving into thin air.

The real Sally was already out of the swarm's reach.

"Too close... Yikes!"

A root had shot up from underfoot.

With her current stats, one hit would kill her.

She couldn't afford to stop for an instant. Dodging the roots, she kept close watch on her surroundings.

Three trees with red fruit. Definitely all treants.

"Fire Ball!"

Treants weren't the most mobile of monsters, so the fire spell struck the trunk easily, setting it aflame.

The treant's roar of anger echoed through the woods.

"Eep! Maybe that was a bad idea!"

That cry was attracting more monsters. Sally's Presence Detect II could sense them coming.

"Mirage!"

She sent a fake running back toward the spring.

This successfully baited the beetles, but no such luck with the spiders. They were still coming right at her—must be some sort of skill.

"Saw through it, huh? Slash!"

Two strikes mid-dodge.

Their HP certainly went down, but it was still at 70 percent. She didn't have time to stop and finish the job.

"Crap...the treants are bad enough...!"

Sally was facing an alarming number of foes, and they were all taking different approaches.

The spiders in particular had pretty high Agility. Almost as high as Sally's.

This made sense—this quest was specifically designed for high-Agility builds.

"Oceanic!"

A thin film of water spread outward from her feet. The pursuing spiders charged right into it, and their numbers thinned.

"Slash! ...Wind Cutter!"

Slicing her way through treant roots and branches, Sally raced onward.

She was slowly gaining ground on the spiders.

But this was really taking its toll on her nerves.

If she slowed for an instant, she'd get caught—but this was a forest. There were trees in her way, brush underfoot, and no telling what path she should take.

If she tripped, she'd instantly be in serious trouble.

She heard a buzzing in her ears and glanced backward.

"More beetles? ...*Oh crap*...!"

There were three *main* types of monster in these woods.

And one more type you almost never encountered.

There was a giant dragonfly on her heels.

The Wind Dragonfly.

As the name suggested, this monster used wind magic to propel itself forward, flying so fast, it was like the trees didn't exist.

"What rotten luck! Holy crap! Wind Cutter!"

She sent wind blades over her shoulder. A warning shot.

She couldn't afford to stop and fight. Her only option was to outrun it. But it was gaining steadily.

High-level wind magic was slicing through the air around Sally, whooshing past her ears. She used trees as shields, dodged the rest, and activated Oceanic again to make the spiders back off.

Sleep Beetles came in from the right, but Mirage distracted them. Still, as she ran, she found herself surrounded once more.

Sally started to worry.

"Spiders in front, treants on the left—guess I'm going that way!"

She was using every scrap of info Presence Detect II gave her to plot the best route.

She found the thickest clump of trees, anything to slow the dragonfly down. Three treants ahead. Naturally, she couldn't afford to engage.

"Mirage!"

The treants were easily fooled. Dozens of pointed branches shot toward her duplicate, running it through.

Certain they'd scored a kill, the treants let out a sinister cackle.

"Thanks!" Sally said, relieved. "Huge help!"

It wasn't Sally they'd stabbed.

It was one of the dragonfly's wings.

The dragonfly had not expected this attack and had completely failed to dodge.

The damaged wing slowed it substantially.

Sally put even more distance between herself and the monsters.

The dragonfly flung wind magic after her, and spells screeched past on either side, but this last desperate attack never stood a chance of hitting her.

"Haah...haah...I made it! Haah! This might have been the most exhausting one yet!"

Sally was outside the log cabin.

It had taken her fifty-two minutes. Just barely in time.

She opened the cabin door.

"I'm back!"

"Oh! There you are. A relief to see you safe and sound."

She'd nearly died a dozen times, so her smile was a little strained, but the old man just kept chattering away.

"Hmm... I suppose I oughtta thank you. Wait here a moment."

He got up and took a scroll out of a drawer.

"This'll teach you the Superspeed skill. I'm sure it'll come in handy. Please take it."

As he spoke, he blurred...and was gone.

"I no longer need it," said a voice behind her.

Sally spun around. There stood the old man, grinning like he'd pulled off the best prank.

"Heh-heh...diligence pays dividends."

"R-right!" Sally said. She left the log cabin behind.

Armed with her new power.

A week hunting new skills flew by, and it was time for the second event. Sally and Maple met up in the second zone town.

"Whew! My first event! Getting a bit nervous," Sally admitted. She tried stretching a bit.

"It's packed again!" Maple said. "Is everyone joining in?"

"Probably. The benefits are really worth it… Oh, here we go."

A stir ran through the crowd.

A crackle emerged from the speakers, and an announcer's voice rang out.

"Let the second event begin!"

As the crowd roared, curtains rose.

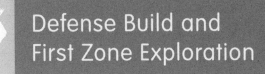

Defense Build and First Zone Exploration

While Maple and Sally were at the underground lake, Sally spent a great deal of time honing her Swimming skill, preparing for the boss fight. But going there wasn't the only reason they logged in. The gear Maple wanted required a number of other materials, and they both wanted to do a little sightseeing.

Once they'd obtained a solid quantity of scales from fishing and diving, they headed elsewhere, searching for the rest of the materials.

"Sally, what next? Where do we start?"

"Hmm… Well, I only just started playing. You've been around longer than I have, so I was planning on following you."

"I actually haven't done much exploring, either. Everywhere I try and go is so far away, and I don't want to spend the whole game session just *walking* somewhere."

The field and towns weren't excessively large. Maple's walking speed was just well below the norm.

But that was certainly a good reason to leave most of the map unexplored.

"Then wanna tour the place with me? Let's start with this town. Maybe the materials the shops are selling will be what you need."

"Okay! That sounds good!"

Maple nodded happily, and the two began walking through the crowded first zone village.

The base material for Maple's gear was the pile of scales they'd gathered at the underground lake, but she wanted to decorate it and needed blue materials for that.

So they were on a quest for materials of that color.

"Guess we should start close at hand!"

"Fair enough."

The shop they entered was run by an NPC and sold a variety of accessories.

It was all a bit pricey for new players, but they sold not only rings and necklaces but individual gems.

"They're pretty, but...not quite what I had in mind."

"Yeah...let's try somewhere else, Maple."

They put down the accessories they'd been examining and left the shop.

"Maybe accessory shops aren't the right place to look," Sally said.

"Hmm...then where else?" Maple asked.

"Maybe a quest reward? Or somewhere out in the field?"

It was often faster to just gather things yourself, like they had at the lake.

"But I don't know where to start!"

Maple only knew the places she'd been and was only familiar with quests where the unlock condition was a defense skill she'd wanted.

She knew a lot about a select few things and almost nothing about anything else.

And this unbalanced knowledge base included absolutely nothing about blue materials.

Since Sally had traveled quite a bit collecting skills, she probably knew more about the map than Maple did.

"Guess we'd better gather intel first, then."

"Fair enough!"

They headed for the board Maple had often used, scanning the monster drops for anything that dropped something blue.

"Dye…isn't really right. What about this, though?"

Maple leaned in to read what Sally was pointing at.

Was this what she was looking for?

"Yeah, let's try that!"

"Cool. Lemme make sure I know where this is. We got what we need?"

The info on the board made it clear this monster didn't use any status effects or have especially strong attacks.

They figured they'd be fine with Maple guarding and Sally chipping away at the enemy, as per usual.

In the unlikely event they did take serious damage, they had enough potions that they didn't need to worry about getting wiped out.

"It's in the forest northwest of town."

"Forest, ho!"

And off they went.

Outside the town, Maple took off her gear and hopped aboard Sally, who set off running.

If she tried walking normally and this material turned out to be no good, they'd have no time to try anywhere else.

This strategy allowed them to compensate for Maple's sluggishness—they'd come up with it when Sally first joined the game and they started visiting the lake.

"You're so fast!"

"You're just slow, Maple."

They passed a few players on the way, and then the Sally Express dropped Maple off at their destination.

During the first event, Maple had defeated a lot of players in a pretty outlandish way and done well enough to reach the podium. She was famous to begin with.

For her to be spotted riding another player around the map with her already budding reputation... Well, that got people talking.

Neither of them realized this.

"Thanks, Sally!" Maple said. As soon as she hit the ground, she put her gear back on, then did a few stretches.

"Mm. Let's find these monsters."

The intel said they weren't particularly rare, so if the two of them looked around a bit, the assumption was that they would find them soon enough.

"Farther in, you think?"

"Yep. This place is pretty far out, but nothing here gives a lot of XP, so I doubt we'll have much competition. We can take our time."

They headed off into the forest.

But of course, the forest had plenty of monsters they *weren't* looking for.

And they couldn't just ignore them.

"Sally, hide behind me."

"Right."

Maple held her shield up, advancing.

Her ultimate move, the shield that consumed everything! It took care of every threat from the fore.

"Maple, above you!"

"Above?!"

Maple looked up just in time to see a green-furred monkey dropping directly toward her. It kicked her right in the face!

"Yikes!"

She let out a yelp but naturally took no damage.

The monkey was now clinging to her head, attacking like crazy, but to Maple, this was no worse than being tickled.

"Slash!"

A dagger bit into its side, causing the monkey to switch targets and instead launch itself at Sally.

But this attack was doomed to fail.

"Where'd it go?!" Maple said, swinging around. Her shield clipped the monkey's feet, consuming the lower half of it.

"Wow, nice—accident, right?"

"Ah-ha-ha, kinda obvious, huh?"

"You had no clue where it was. Best to keep an eye on the trees above."

"Yeah. Will do."

Maple thrust her shield directly upward a few times, practicing.

"We can sell their drops for money later. I don't think they'll help with your gear."

Sally was stuffing the monkey's green fur into her inventory.

This material wasn't worth that much, but everything added up eventually.

As long as they had space in their inventories, it couldn't hurt to hoover everything up.

*   *   *

Fending off the occasional attack from shrubberies or the trees above, they moved forward another ten minutes.

The leaves around them were a deeper shade of green now.

"I think we're here. Maple, you can put that down now."

"Oh?"

Maple had been holding her great shield over her head like an umbrella, but now she went back to a more orthodox stance.

The monsters dropping from above had landed on her shield, which, in turn, had become their final resting place.

"Let's at least find one of these things."

"Yeah."

They inched forward, scanning their surroundings.

Sally, in particular, was turning this way and that, not missing a single waggling bush.

"There!"

"Where?"

By the time Maple turned toward her, Sally was already running.

"Slash!"

Her dagger raked the bush, knocking a four-inch spider into the air.

It had an obsidian-like body, but Sally could see its eyes glitter like blue gems.

"Whoops!"

Maple had tried to run forward, shield aloft, but had tripped on a tree root and wiped out...just as the spider hit her—right on the shield. Devour kicked in.

"You okay?"

"Ugh, yeah. Thanks."

Sally helped Maple up.

Maple patted her armor down, brushing the dust off. She looked around.

"Where'd it go?"

"You killed it. But it didn't drop anything."

"Oh…guess we'd better try again!"

They moved around the silent forest—not even a single bird singing—and slew another ten spiders without getting a single item.

"This is an awfully low drop rate."

"The resale value is pretty high, so that's expected. What do you think? Wanna split up? They're easy enough to beat if we spot 'em first."

These spiders didn't have much HP, and Sally could locate them with her innate detection skills, so they didn't pose much of a threat to her, while Maple was largely defeating them by simply walking around.

She readily agreed to Sally's plan, and they set out, hoping to gather more efficiently.

"I'll message you in twenty, then."

"Yeah! Let's do this!"

Sally vanished into the brush, and Maple started hunting spiders again.

Sadly, Sally had been the one finding everything. On her own, Maple was coming up empty.

"Right! Taunt!"

When Maple activated her skill, a spider shot out of the nearby underbrush. A blue magic circle appeared, and it fired a spell at Maple.

"Got one!"

The spider was on the ground, so all Maple had to do was flatten it with her shield.

Unlike Sally's daggers, this mystery shield could eliminate them in a single blow.

Maple picked her shield up again and checked the ground, but once again—no drops.

"It'll be a while before I can use that again, so I guess I'll just wander around."

Maple pushed her way through the rustling bushes and checked the trees above. No luck.

She was beginning to think she'd never find any without using Taunt.

"Okay, one more time, then…"

"Maple!"

"Huh?"

Sally's voice came from deep in the woods.

It hadn't been twenty minutes yet.

It was too soon for her to call.

"I'd better hurry!"

Maple ran off toward the voice.

She came hurtling out of the brush to find Sally engaged in heated combat with a spider three times the size of the others.

"Maple, help! This thing is hella dodgy!"

Sally was swinging her daggers, effortlessly dodging every attack the spider made, so Maple figured the monster was probably thinking the exact same thing.

"Taunt!" she cried. But it didn't seem to affect the spider. Its attention stayed focused on Sally. "Fine, then. Sally! Run toward me!"

They were still a fair distance apart.

"Got it!"

Sally turned her back on the spider and broke into a run.

The spider quickly followed, and they both whizzed past Maple.

"Hydra!"

Up against the gushing flow of poison, the spider was ridiculously tiny and all too feeble. It drowned in a sea of poison before it even caught up with Sally.

"O-overkill..."

"Don't step in it, Sally! I'll see if it dropped anything."

Maple went squelching through the noxious pond she'd made. She found something blue and glittering...and dripping with poison.

She bent down, picked it up, wiped off the toxic sludge, and revealed a blue sphere the size of a Ping-Pong ball—an impressive-looking gemstone.

"Oh, a drop! That's it, Maple!"

"We finally got one! And it's pretty, too. Well worth the hard work!"

Maple rolled it around her hand a moment longer, then put it in her inventory.

"Large Spider's Blue Eye, it's called. That was an eye?!"

"Yep! The kinda material you only get in games. Looks like the size and drop rates are different depending on the size of the spider... Wanna pick up a few more off the little ones, too?"

"Yeah...if we can, I mean. I'd like to?"

"Then let's go. We got plenty of time."

Just in case more large spiders showed up, they went back to working together. A smaller one scuttled past.

"Slash! Haah!"

Sally reacted instantly, knocking the spider into the air, then slashing it several times like a circus performer, carving its HP away without giving it a chance to escape.

"Oh, a drop!"

She snatched up the blue orb and tossed it to Maple.

"W-wow...I wonder if I can do that?"

"Kinda hard with a shield...and I've been practicing a lot in-game. That's why."

"Hmm...then okay. Dual wielding sure does look cool!"

"Heh-heh...thanks."

They didn't encounter any more of the rare larger spiders but killed another few dozen small spiders, finding two more gems.

"I think that's enough," Maple said, leaning against a nearby tree. "I'm just using them as an accent, after all. Thanks, Sally."

"Tired?"

"A bit, yeah. I haven't really done any prolonged hunts like this."

If you weren't used to something, it wore you out fast.

Maple hadn't moved around much during the first event, and when she had, she'd made sure to rest after.

So this hunt had been one of the first times she'd really been on the go this long.

"You'll get used to it soon enough. I did!"

"I'll take your word for it."

They stepped out of the woods into the sunlight. They both stretched.

"Want me to carry you home?"

"I accept this generous offer!"

"When we get back, we should do some actual sightseeing. You've got the materials you needed, after all."

"Sounds good!"

"Cool. Then hop on board!"

Maple removed her gear and attached herself to Sally.

Sally took off, moving far faster than she ever could in the real world, headed straight for town.

They made it all the way back without being forced into any fights.

"Here we are! Where to next, Maple?"

"You pick, Sally."

"Put me on the spot, why don't you? Um, why don't we start by grabbing something to eat? In-game food won't impact our real-world wallets, and some players are even running their own restaurants."

Most players were focused on grinding levels, but there were plenty who played the game on their own terms.

"Let's do that, then! I could go for some dessert."

"Me too! Let's take a look around."

To ease their fatigue…

…and treat their tongues.

They set out in search of sweets and a player-run shop.

◆□◆□◆□◆□◆

After wandering the streets for a bit, they found a shop with a subdued brown exterior but a tantalizingly classy feel. The flowers out front must have been watered recently; the light caught the beads of water on them, glittering.

"Maple, wanna go here?"

"Yes, let's! These all sound good," Maple said, eyeing the chalkboard menu outside.

"Cool. After you!" Sally held the door open, then followed Maple in.

It was a modest-size interior, and there were already several other players here.

They glanced up when the door opened, spotted Maple, and looked surprised.

Maple had garnered a ton of attention in the first event and, thanks to her distinctive armor, had continued to stand out ever since—so most players knew who she was.

Thanks to the awards ceremony, people assumed she was a top player, and everywhere she went, people noticed.

Picking up on the tension immediately, Sally turned to Maple and said, "Man, you're totally famous."

"I—I am?"

Maple seemed utterly baffled by it.

She hadn't even noticed all the looks she was getting.

"Never mind. Wanna sit over there? Looks open."

Sally pointed to a table by the wall.

"Sure. That seems like a nice spot."

They sat down and scanned the menus.

Something was bothering Sally, and she finally put her finger on it.

"Oh! Okay. Maple, you're wearing heavy armor! Doesn't feel right in a shop like this."

"...Good point."

Maple glanced around at the other players.

Everyone here today was wearing robes or other lighter gear, so she really stood out.

Naturally, this game had plenty of players who wore armor every bit as bulky as Maple's.

Situations like this might not crop up often, but at the moment, Maple was seriously considering buying herself a non-armor outfit.

"Maybe we should do some shopping after."

"That could work. For now, let's order something."

"Yeah—lemme go through the menu first."

Maple picked the menu up again, leafing through it. This shop's menu primarily offered re-creations of real-world desserts. Shortcake, vanilla ice cream—it was easy to guess what most options would taste like. Sally ordered a strawberry tart, and Maple, a slice of chocolate cake.

While they waited, their conversation turned to the future.

"When's the next event? Hope it's something we can do together."

"Yeah, I'd love to run an event with you, Sally."

It had been a long wait, but at last they could play together.

And both of them wanted to spend as much time as possible helping each other out and having fun together.

"If it's the same format as the first event, that won't be an option."

"Yeah...I don't really want to fight you."

"Oh?" Sally said, surprised.

"I mean, I don't think I could win," Maple admitted.

"I'm not so sure... I mean, I definitely wouldn't make it easy for you, but..."

As she spoke, their orders arrived.

The strawberry tart gave off a sweet scent, and the vivid colors sang a bright song of spring.

The chocolate cake was a calm brown, with a slightly darker chocolate coating.

They each took a bite.

"Oh, that *is* good! I bet this would be really expensive in the real world," Maple said, savoring the slightly bitter tang.

"Yeah, it's nice getting to eat such fancy desserts like this. Yours looks good, too!"

"Want a bite?"

Sally considered this for a moment.

"...Nah, I'll just order my own."

She flagged a server down, ordered a slice of cake for herself, and then started in on her tart.

"Maybe I should get more, too..."

You could order as much as you liked in-game, and it wouldn't cost you a dime of real money.

And you didn't have to worry about calories.

"Maple! This looks good, too!"

"Hmm...maybe I should go for that."

"Totally!"

They enjoyed all the desserts they wanted.

"Come again!"

An hour and a half later, they finally left the shop.

""..........""

As they stepped out, a blue panel popped up in front of each of them. Their eyes locked on one corner.

Where their in-game money was displayed.

"We...spent a lot."

"Well...we ordered a lot."

That shop wasn't exactly cheap, either.

They'd seen the numbers on the menu but had gotten a little carried away.

Perhaps they'd splurged a bit too much.

"Um, so what now?" Maple asked.

"Sightseeing? I certainly saw some lovely places out in the field."

She'd run across them while gathering skills.

And Sally had found info about even more beautiful views completely unrelated to skills or useful items.

"Somewhere we can go anytime... Out west, there's an area with a perpetual sunset. And there's a nighttime-only zone up north."

"Those sound good! If you're up for it, Sally."

She meant if they had time to get there but also if Sally was willing to carry her.

That was the only way they were visiting these places in a reasonable time frame.

But since the field tourism was her idea, Sally had absolutely no qualms about giving Maple a ride.

"Wish they had bicycles."

"We'll have to wait for them to patch those in. But I bet horses are more likely..."

"Erp. I'm not sure I could ever ride a horse..."

Fueled by desserts, they set out into the field.

And along the way, they planned to fight a few monsters and earn back some of the money they'd spent.

Maple had already forgotten her desire to buy a non-armor outfit, so it would likely be quite some time before she bought anything more touristy.

◆□◆□◆□◆□◆

They headed west across the field. Sally's spells kept most monsters at bay, and those that attacked anyway were rewarded with a Hydra to the face.

"You're unmatched out here, huh?"

"Eh-heh-heh! You think so?"

"I've gotta catch up! Fire Ball!"

Sally's fire magic couldn't hope to compete with Maple's gushing poison, but each spell scored a clean hit on her targets.

It wasn't flashy, but you could clearly see the work she'd put into mastering the technique.

"Not too shabby."

"Sally, are we almost there?"

"It's not much farther. You can see it up ahead!"

Maple squinted at the horizon.

She could definitely see *something* up there.

"That's...not a sunset, though."

"Nope. Just a landmark."

Sally sped up, racing toward it like the last spurt of a race.

"We're here!"

Maple hopped down off Sally's back, put her gear back on, and looked around.

Stone pillars carved to different heights were placed at even intervals, forming a circle.

It was very Stonehenge-y.

At the center of the circle was a mark, like something had burned there. That was ominous.

"What now?"

"This."

Sally strode confidently to the center and stopped there.

"Fire Ball!"

She dropped the spell at her feet, and the charred mark glowed red.

"Come on, Maple!"

"Er, uh...right..."

Maple trotted over to her. Surrounded by stone columns, they stood waiting, watching the changes unfold.

The red light at their feet grew darker and spread outward like a spider's web, connecting to the towering stones around.

The fiery red spread up the stone, making them glow like pillars of flame.

"Almost... Now!"

"Whoa!"

Everything went white, and Maple closed her eyes, raising a hand to shield them.

The girls vanished like a fire burning out. The red glow slowly faded, leaving only the stone circle and the scorch mark at the center.

With no clue what was going on, Maple had screwed her eyes shut, but when she felt the wind on her face, she slowly opened them again.

"Wow..."

A gentle breeze ran through her hair.

The view around them had changed completely.

Maple and Sally were on top of a hill.

A path wound down the slope, and fields of sunflowers spread out on either side. In the distance was an ocean, the water dyed red by the setting sun.

Behind that was the sunset itself. Silhouetted against it were floating castle spires and dragons in flight—this definitely wasn't the real world.

There was no one else around, just the whistling of the wind.

The cool breeze carried the scent of sunflowers and the sea.

"You definitely don't get to see this every day."

Listening closely, they could hear waves lapping against the shore.

"Mm! It's pretty but…a bit lonely, too, don't you think?"

"Yeah, maybe."

They walked down the path to the ocean. The sunflowers lining the path were taller than either of them, so once they set out, they were completely hidden from view.

"Should we take one with us?" Maple asked, poking a sunflower stalk.

"Don't think we can. Seems like they're indestructible objects. We'll just have to drink in the sunset and then go. You can come back anytime if you learn fire magic, though."

"I'll have to be on the lookout."

Maple tried to remember if she'd read about any fire skills she could actually learn, but so far, she hadn't come across anything of the sort.

They'd gone far enough now that they could clearly see a strip of sand by the water's edge.

The waves crashed against the fine sand, and the light of the sunset made the spray gleam.

They walked out into the surf and found two things lying there.

"What are these?"

Maple picked one up and examined it.

It was an item called the Madder Pearl Oyster.

The shell was as red as the name implied, and when it opened, it revealed a single pink-hued pearl within.

The item description merely said it could be sold for a good price to NPC vendors.

"Basically a souvenir, huh? I dunno if it can be used as a material, but at least we can get some cash."

Sally picked up the other oyster, looking it over.

The color so perfectly matched the view that looking at it would definitely bring back memories.

"Maybe I'll just treasure it!" Maple said, putting it in her inventory.

"Yeah, same here." Sally nodded. "Seems a waste to sell it."

She put hers away, too. They could take it out anytime and feel like they were here once more.

"Sally, can we wander around a little longer?"

"Sure. I'm not feeling the need to leave, either. It's a long time before we can access the night-only zone, so we'll have to log out for a while anyway. We can take our time here."

"Good! Then let's do that."

They were both feeling like lingering awhile.

Maple sat down on the sand and pointed up at the floating castle.

"Think we'll be able to go somewhere like that one day?"

"Not sure. I've cleared a dungeon like that in a different game."

Maple looked jealous.

"We'll make it there eventually," Sally said. "Together. I bet you could beat those dragons easily."

"Whaaa...? I don't think so."

Someday, they'd get the chance to visit that castle. They were both looking forward to it.

"I'm glad you're enjoying the game, Maple."

"Heh-heh! I am! It's great."

Maple smiled happily.

The setting sun shone down until they left the area—and after they were gone.

Outside the eternal sunset area, they both logged out, agreeing to meet up at the starting square.

When Maple logged back in, she headed over to the fountain. At night, the town's streets were bathed in the glow of the streetlights. There were fewer NPCs, so the feel of the town was noticeably different. Maple looked around, searching for Sally.

"Where is she...? There!"

"Oh, there you are, Maple!"

"Let's get going!"

"Sure. We head north!"

They went out the north side, assumed their usual travel style, and off they went.

"There are monsters that get stronger at night and others that only appear after dark, so keep an eye out, Maple."

"Okay! Will do!"

Some monsters were nocturnal, while others only appeared during the day.

"Oh, speak of the devil..."

"Er, what? Yikes!"

Something floated silently down from above, hit Maple in the forehead, and then floated back into the sky.

Even with everything but her short sword stashed in her inventory, Maple's defense was so high, this sneak attack did no damage at all, but it wasn't going away, either.

"Maple, get down a moment."

"Sure thing!"

Maple hopped off Sally and moved a few steps back.

"Taunt!" she said, forcing the monster to target her. She then reequipped her armor as fast as she could.

The monsters came down to their level, making futile attacks.

There were several of them now.

"Double Slash!"

Sally's daggers struck one of these monsters in the back.

"An owl?"

Sally had knocked it to the ground, and they got a clear look at it.

Sally stabbed it in the back with her dagger, vanquishing the remainder of its HP.

But most of the owls were still high above.

"Maple, send a dragon up there."

"Got it! Hydra!"

Maple raised her black blade toward the heavens, deploying a large purple magic circle.

Sally started running away at top speed.

She had no other option.

A few seconds later, the ground around Maple turned to hell on earth.

The three dragon heads shot upward, swallowing and demolishing a bunch of the owls around Maple.

The dragon split apart in the upper atmosphere, and the poison fell back down in clumps far too large to call *rain*.

This second wave of poison successfully took out all the remaining owls.

A series of splats hit the ground around Maple, dyeing it a toxic purple.

"Maple!" Sally called from a considerably safer distance. "I can't get anywhere near you! You'll have to come to me!"

Maple took off her gear again and ran over to Sally.

"That was easier than I thought!" she said.

"That's pretty typical for you, though. If there were monsters lying everywhere who could actually give you trouble, nobody else would survive long."

"Really?"

"Pretty much just a handful of the top players."

Anything that could dish out enough damage to bother Maple would kill any other player in one or two hits.

"Let's keep moving. If we run into any more owls, we can pull that same trick again."

"Roger that!"

They plunged into a forest, taking the shortest route to their destination.

It would normally be hard to walk at all in a dark forest. But the woods were aglow with an uncanny illumination. Some came from two-inch-long fireflies perched on trunks and bushes. The rest came from luminescent moss that lit the ground at their feet. There were lots of shrubs and thorns that required careful footwork.

That meant Sally couldn't carry Maple any farther.

"Gear on...good!"

Maple took the lead.

If Sally was in front, she could detect danger ahead.

But if she missed a threat, she might well end up dead.

Maple, on the other hand, could walk headfirst into a trap and break the trap instead.

Everything worked exactly the way the designers had intended, but it was no match for her.

She just soaked it all.

And Maple had a long-range attack.

That meant having Maple in front was always the best plan.

"Lemme know if anything happens!"

"Sure! Watch for briars!"

Even as she spoke, a thorny briar rose up from the ground in front of Maple, attacking.

"Haah!"

But she just raised her shield, and it literally took a bite out of the briar.

What was left of it shattered into light fragments.

"That's so strong."

"I know, right? It's cool! I like it!"

It was probably stronger than any weapon in the game.

"Keep it up, then!"

"Chugging along!"

Unfettered by any more briar patches, they easily defeated a few enemy bats and reached their destination.

"Here?"

Maple pointed in front.

"Yep, here."

They were outside a cave entrance, maybe seven feet high.

An entrance that promised thrills and the prospect of treasure within.

Sally fished a torch out of her inventory and lit it to peer inside.

"Stairs that go up. Pretty narrow, so mind staying in the lead?"

"No prob."

"Cool. Let's head in! Apparently, there are some beautiful sights in here."

They stepped into the cave.

In search of the views within.

The stairs were pretty steep. They were hewn directly out of the rock and had no handrail, so it was a pretty challenging climb.

If any monsters appeared, Maple couldn't exactly unleash a poison dragon on a narrow stairway with Sally right behind, so her short sword didn't do much good.

She'd elected to take the torch from Sally, allowing her to dual wield.

They climbed for ten full minutes.

They reached the top without any monster encounters and found themselves beneath a sky filled with far more stars than were ever visible in the real world. A pleasant breeze ruffled their hair.

"That was quite a climb—where are we?"

"It's too dark to see, but there are cliffs all around us. Be careful."

"Cliffs? Oh, you're right!"

They were standing at the top of a pillar maybe ten yards in diameter.

A formation like this would certainly be visible by day, and Maple was pretty sure she'd seen it before.

"No one else here? That's a stroke of luck."

"I-is that…?"

Paying very close attention to where she walked, Maple moved to the center of the pillar—she'd spotted a light.

There lay a wooden table. It had elaborate decorations carved around the edges, but the top was perfectly smooth. It was very strange seeing something like this outdoors.

There were two chairs placed on opposite sides, two wine-glasses, two sets of silverware, and two lovely white plates. In the center of the table was a candelabra, the candles unlit.

"Sally, want to sit down?"

"Yeah—I hear if you do, *something* happens."

This time, she wasn't sure what.

She'd just seen a few vague comments on message boards saying something neat happened if you came here with someone.

"Then on the count of three?" Maple suggested.

"Why not?"

""One, two—three!""

As one, they pulled the chairs out and sat down.

Right as they did, there was a *fwoom* as the candles lit up.

And before their very eyes, the wineglasses began to levitate.

As they gaped at this, two indigo threads descended from the starry sky.

Each poured itself into one of the wineglasses.

When the glasses were half-full, they floated back to the table's surface.

"What the...?"

"Huh..."

Inside the glasses were miniature starry skies.

Like the skies above, stars sparkled, clouds drifted past, and between those clouds floated a crescent moon.

Looking up made them feel like they were adrift in a sea of celestial bodies. Looking down made it feel like they were being sucked into their glasses.

While they were gasping at this sight, it was the plates' turn to take flight.

The candles sputtered, and a tiny flame flew to each plate.

These spun in place, forming spheres above the plates' centers.

As they watched, two drops fell from the sky, wreathed in pale light.

As they neared the plates, the light left the drops, forming softly glowing little yellow spheres. Like the fire, the drop hovered above the plate's surface.

Three spheres in all, one red, one blue, and one yellow.

The plates settled back on the table, and a sign appeared between the girls—where each could see. It had the name of the dish written on it.

"'Miniature Sky'?"

"'Please enjoy'?"

Maple and Sally exchanged glances, then picked up their forks and knives and started eating.

"It's like nothing I've ever eaten..."

"It's good...I think? What's your take, Maple?"

"Er, um... It's like I'm eating strawberries and tangerines and apples all at once? If that makes sense."

"Yeah, it kinda does...," Sally said, nodding.

It was sweet but also tart. Warm but nice and cold.

It didn't taste like anything they would have been able to eat in the real world, Maple thought.

"And this drink..."

Sally took a sip of the starry sky.

It fizzed in her mouth, the liquid sensation vanishing.

"Sally?! Y-your hair's glowing!"

Maple had looked up after eating the red and blue spheres and noticed a dramatic change.

"Huh?" Sally blinked, then pulled a hand mirror out of her inventory to check.

Her hair was gleaming like it had stars in it.

"Mm? Maple, your eyes changed color."

She handed Maple her mirror.

Maple peered into it and found her left eye was red and her right eye blue.

"Whaaaa...? Are they gonna turn back...?"

"G-good question..."

After their very strange dinner beneath the starry sky, the girls rose to leave. Their hair still sparkling, their eyes still different colors.

As they stood, a message appeared on the card.

Sally read it aloud.

"'Thank you for coming. Tonight's meal had too many hidden flavors and was a failure! But please, do come again. Take this by way of apology.'"

Two bottles appeared on the table.

Sally picked them both up.

"What are those?" Maple asked.

"'Bottled Starry Sky.'"

"Wh-what do they do?"

Sally cleared her throat and then explained...

"'The messed-up chef messed up! Do not open! You actually can't open it. But it is nice to look at!'...it says."

"W-wow..."

Maple took one bottle from her and put it in her inventory.

They might not be able to open it, but even if she could, she'd probably take that warning to heart and leave it shut tight.

"Should we come again?" Maple asked.

"If the chef gets better at cooking, sure."

"Ah-ha-ha...I don't see that happening."

It had been a strange meal but a fascinating one. They'd remember it for a long time.

They left the restaurant behind.

In later days, they saw a forum post claiming that on rare occasions, the chef's dishes were a success. Maybe they'd try their luck again someday.

A few days after their strange starlit meal, their hair and eyes finally returned to normal. Maple had logged in alone and was wandering around town.

She had somewhere she needed to go.

*   *   *

"Um...was it this way?" She was wandering back and forth, feeling like this town was a bit too big for someone as slow as she was. "Oh! There it is."

She finally found the building she was looking for and hustled toward it. She opened the door and went in.

"Oh, hey! It's been far too long."

"Right? I'm finally back, Iz."

The shop hadn't changed a bit.

Iz was behind the counter, arranging merchandise on the display rack.

Maple had finally gathered the money and materials and was here to place an order.

She showed Iz what she had.

Iz examined the materials.

"You've got enough money, but...hmm..."

"Wh-what?"

"These materials alone won't give you much of a VIT buff or make the equipment all that durable. I saw how you fought in the last event, but...based on that, I'd want to add a few more materials, here."

Neither Maple nor Sally had dabbled in crafting at all, so when they'd gathered materials, it hadn't occurred to them to worry about durability.

And they'd had no idea what materials would improve quality.

At this rate, the results would be a little lacking, even for sub-equipment.

"Um...so what else do I need?"

Maple wanted the best gear she could manage.

"...Just a moment."

Iz began going through the extra materials she'd need, one at a time.

*　　*　　*

After explaining the last material, Iz started to wrap things up.

Then an idea struck her. "Oh! One more thing," she said. This was about the white crystals. "Gathering those requires some high-level skills, which I'm assuming you don't have... I'm right, aren't I? In that case..."

Iz nodded to herself, mulling it over.

Once she'd straightened it out in her mind, she began explaining it to Maple.

"Getting those materials requires going all the way to the back of a cave filled with monsters. You can collect a lot at once, so I usually hire guards to take me there and back, but my stock's run out at the moment. So..."

Iz offered Maple a proposition.

In return for escorting her to the cave, Iz would give Maple some of what she gathered and offer a discount on the price for making the gear.

Maple saw no reason to turn this offer down.

She accepted at once.

"If you've got time, we can go now," Iz said.

"Uh, sure thing!"

"Great! And thank you."

And so they agreed to explore the cave together.

Maple left first, and Iz joined her a few minutes later, once she was ready.

She flipped the sign on the door to CLOSED and then turned toward Maple.

"Shall we?" she said.

"Sure!"

Maple started walking with Iz at her side.

Iz, however, was much faster.

Crafters used STR for blacksmith work, but gathering skills was based on DEX and AGI, so they had to keep those stats at a decent level, too.

Iz had wound up with a focused, balanced build.

When she realized Maple was lagging behind, Iz slowed down, matching her pace.

"You're totally different in combat…or no, I guess not."

On the event stream, Maple had been ridiculously strong, mowing other players down left and right. Looking at her now, it was hard to imagine that.

But then Iz remembered the look on Maple's face as she'd fought and changed her mind.

Right now or in mid-combat, Maple had clearly just been having a great time.

What gear would be best for her…?

How could Iz help her have an even better time? What could she make for her?

Iz pondered this question as she and Maple left the town behind.

Out in the field, there were monsters trying to interfere with their progress.

Their already slow pace slowed even further. Maple made for a very strange sort of guard, but she successfully prevented anything from attacking Iz.

First, Maple used Taunt to make sure all monsters targeted her instead. Wolves then leaped at her from behind, biting the back of Maple's neck, and their weight knocked her over.

"Eeeep! H-hngg… Let go!"

Maple shook her head, trying to get the wolf off. To no avail.

Eventually, she managed to dislodge the wolf by falling over backward onto it.

Once it let go, the wolf stood no chance. It didn't take long for Maple's shield to swallow it up.

Iz was used to guards protecting their client while carefully managing how much damage they took themselves.

Maple didn't really bother with the latter half.

Seeing this in person really drove home how broken Maple was. Just watching her was making Iz tired.

"No wonder she did so well..."

Maple coming in third definitely hadn't been a fluke.

It took them a while, but eventually they reached the cave.

The entrance was on the side of a mountain, and the path wound slowly farther in. It was quite dark, even in daylight.

The ground was slightly damp, but the path was relatively wide. Four adults could walk side by side.

"Careful."

"Okay!"

Iz pulled a lantern out of her inventory, lighting their way.

This made it easy to see where they were going, and if they kept an eye on their feet, they were unlikely to trip themselves up.

They headed down a gentle slope.

Maple had her shield and short sword brandished. Iz was toting a blacksmithing hammer, just in case.

"Keep one eye on the ceiling. We should be encountering something soon."

"Okay, the ceiling?"

Maple looked up just in time for something sharp to shatter on her forehead.

Surprised, she closed her eyes, crouching with her shield raised like an umbrella.

After a moment, she calmed down and looked around. She saw a foot-long lizard with its tail stuck in a pointed rock.

But the tail rock had shattered into pieces all around it.

These lizard monsters clung to the ceiling, falling on players who came along.

But the moment it hit Maple, the soft lizard parts had been no match for the impact, and it had wound up destroying itself.

"Haah!"

Maple pounded her shield on the ground, wiping out the last of the lizard's HP.

"That sure surprised me..."

"...That's *all* it did."

It had scored a clean hit to no avail. These lizards were built for ambush attacks but were helpless against her.

Maybe Maple didn't need to bother watching the ceiling.

"Are there any monsters in here strong enough to beat you? ... Nope."

Iz remembered her last trip here. There were lots of monsters, but none of them seemed like they'd stand a chance against Maple.

If there were any monsters that powerful, none of her other guards would have lasted very long.

"I guess I don't need that many of these...," Iz muttered, taking some HP recovery potions out of her pouch and sticking them back in her inventory. In their place, she put a number of pills that would provide a brief buff to her stats.

If no one needed to heal, there was no point in having potions ready.

"The number of monsters picks up the farther we go," she said. "Good luck!"

"Okay! I think I can handle it."

Maple hefted her shield again and moved forward, watching the floor, ceiling, and walls.

Lots of monsters appeared on their way in.

Many of these threw themselves directly at Maple.

But whether these were goblins, mudmen, or golems…

They all ran right up to her, attacking at close quarters with weapons or arms.

And the moment these struck Maple's great shield, they were sucked into it, like they were falling into a bottomless swamp.

"Whew."

"Thanks. We should be almost there…"

Iz checked the map she'd used last time, verifying their current location.

She'd been through the cave before, and Maple's defense was indomitable, so they were making very good progress.

And since it was a cave, monsters mostly came from the fore, making it much less likely that they'd be surrounded. That meant they made faster progress than in the open field.

As a result, they reached the back without either of them taking damage.

"Found it!"

"This is what we're looking for?" Maple touched the lantern-lit wall.

It was covered in lumpy white ore—the likes of which she hadn't seen on the path in.

"Yep, that's it. Won't be a minute."

Iz took a large pickax out of her inventory and started gathering.

Each time the pickax struck the white ore, an item fell to Iz's feet. After gathering five times, she collected the minerals and moved to the next spot.

There were a number of veins around this ending area, and her goal was to mine each of them.

No monsters spawned here, so she could focus on the task at hand.

Maple was relieved she'd been an effective guard.

"Oh! Don't want any monsters wandering in. Iz! Iz!"

Maple borrowed a lantern from her and stood at the border between the monster area and the gathering zone.

This was her first time guarding anyone. It couldn't hurt to be cautious.

Iz finished mining without incident and joined Maple.

"All done," she said. "Let's head home. We've still got to settle on a design for your gear."

"Yes! Let's have a good return trip!"

Just as before, no monsters in the cave were a match for Maple's shield.

They slowly picked their way back to town, dispatching all monsters foolish enough to come at them.

Paying Iz's shop another visit, they settled down at a table.

The next step was to decide what her order would look like.

This had no effect on function.

But that didn't make it any less important. Some things were more important than stats. Maple thought so anyway.

"So what did you have in mind?"

"Well…well…hmm…"

Maple hadn't really formed all *that* clear a mental image.

She had started with a vague idea that her gear should be white, but that idea hadn't really grown any less vague.

No further details came to mind.

But there was one thing she'd thought about on their adventure, so she decided to start there.

"Today reminded me of something... My shield destroys everything. So I thought it would be a good idea to have a *normal* one."

Iz nodded at this.

Like Maple said, there were times you'd want another approach.

This was the main goal of a secondary loadout.

"Okay...then let's make the shield first. Oh, the more materials you use, the stronger it gets, but that would mean the rest of the set will have to wait."

Maple decided to use the extra items and make a better shield.

She wanted matching armor and a short sword, too, but decided it would be better to have one really good shield than a whole set of mediocre gear.

She knew where and how to get the materials now, so she could always go back if she had to.

Now that they'd settled on only crafting a shield, Maple had to decide on a design.

"I dunno...," she said, clearly at a total loss.

"Well," Iz suggested, "if you're not sure, how about I show you a few shields—see if they give you any ideas? Wait right here."

Iz got up and went to the back. She put a bunch of shields in her inventory and returned to the table.

"Let's go one at a time."

"Okay!"

Iz started showing Maple her shields.

Heavily decorated shields, very simple ones, round shields, square ones.

The more options she saw, the more lost Maple was.

All these shields were handmade by Iz herself.

They were very nice, and that made it extra hard to narrow down.

Just as Maple was reaching peak indecision, she realized there was one shield she definitely liked best.

"Iz, I like this shield!" she said—showing Iz her own black shield.

"Ahhh…I shoulda known. Well, let's start with that design and keep the form factor as similar as we can. That'll make it feel the same to wield."

"That sounds nice!"

They had the biggest piece settled, so Iz moved to drawing up a detailed schematic.

She pulled a contract item out of her inventory, and Maple promised to trade materials and money for a shield.

"I'll let you know once it's done. It'll be a few days."

"Got it! And thank you!"

Maple bowed her head and left the shop.

"Whew…I'm glad that went well."

She'd been a good guard and successfully ordered her shield.

Her goals for the day accomplished, Maple waited breathlessly for the shield's completion.

Maybe half an hour after Maple placed her order, Chrome walked into Iz's shop.

"Oh, Chrome! Here for maintenance?"

"You guessed it."

Chrome pulled his gear out of his inventory, handing it to Iz.

She took it into the back and emerged a short while later. This process restored the gear's durability.

"You sure took a beating this time! Don't break it, ya hear?"

She handed it back to him.

Iz had made all of Chrome's gear for him.

And she hoped it would continue serving him for a long time.

"Yeah, I've been going at it pretty hard. Hoping to do well in the second event, too."

"You getting good results?"

"Not too bad. I'm going hunting again today. Thanks!"

"Sure... Oh, by the way, Chrome. You just missed Maple."

That stopped him in his tracks.

"Oh yeah? Wish I'd come by earlier, then. She ready to order her custom gear already?"

He looked surprised.

Iz told him about their adventure and the shield she'd agreed to make.

"A secondary shield, huh? Makes sense." Chrome nodded. "That black shield of hers is a bit too OP."

As a great shielder himself, he could imagine times when a player just wanted their shield to be a shield.

"Yeah. Well, I'm sure you'll bump into her again somewhere. I see her around town pretty often."

Maple's equipment was incredibly conspicuous, so it was easy to pick her out of a crowd.

The only reason Chrome hadn't seen her was because he'd been out hunting—while Maple had been spending a lot of time sightseeing.

"I'm sure I will. First, I gotta make myself stronger!"

"Good luck."

And with that, Chrome left the shop.

Maple had easily surpassed him, but he wasn't about to give up yet.

The grinding he'd been doing was getting good results, and he headed out to the field to make those better still.

AFTERWORD

To everyone who picked this book up, thank you.

This was only possible with the support of many people and some astonishing coincidences.

The editor who brought me the opportunity to be published—and Koin, who took on illustration duties.

I cannot be grateful enough.

I'm sure some people picking up this book previously read the web novel, while others are entirely new to the series. I'm grateful to both.

I remember when I first started writing novels, it was so clunky and hard to read. I still have a lot of room for improvement, but I feel like I've finally taken that first big step forward.

I Don't Want to Get Hurt, so I'll Max Out My Defense is something I started writing as a change of pace. It was pure coincidence that people noticed, and I remember feeling like the spotlights had suddenly found me.

Everything changed overnight. Things like this really do happen, which proves you should always make hay while the sun shines. I managed to seize the luck that came my way, and I'm holding on to it still.

And it's the readers who've allowed me to continue writing this story.

Your support and corrections. The very fact that you were reading. All of that gave me the fuel I needed to keep going.

Before I knew it, I'd been writing for a full year. That's a long time, but it certainly didn't feel like it.

Like I said, I can't be grateful enough.

But if I keep saying thanks, that's all I'll have room to do, so I think I'd better talk briefly about *Bofuri* itself.

First, about the word itself! *Bofuri* is the first half of the word *defense* and the second half of a Japanese gaming term for extreme builds (translated here as *max out*). With a title this long, you always need a good shortcut, and this one seemed easy to remember.

I'd never picked a nickname before, so…I hope it's working out for everyone.

For this print edition, I was asked to write a new bonus story—another first for me. I had to find ways to expand things without contradicting the original story. This was a real challenge! But the work was worth it, and I think the result shows how much fun they're having in the game.

Finally, on a personal note, it was a long road to get this book published, so I have to reserve some extra-special thanks for the people who were there for me at the start.

* * *

Whoops, I'm back to thanking people! I think I'd better bring an end to this afterword and the first volume of *I Don't Want to Get Hurt, so I'll Max Out My Defense.*

I still value the good fortune that so many people brought me that day.

And if such fortune should come my way once more...

Then perhaps we'll meet again someday.

I'm looking forward to it!

Yuumikan

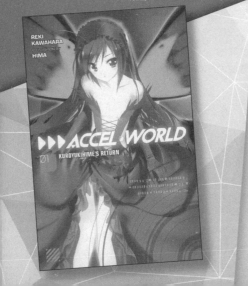

I've Been Killing SLIMES for 300 Years and Maxed Out My Level

It's hard work taking it slow...

After living a painful life as an office worker, Azusa ended her short life by dying from overworking. So when she found herself reincarnated as an undying, unaging witch in a new world, she vows to spend her days stress free and as pleasantly as possible. She ekes out a living by hunting down the easiest targets—the slimes! But after centuries of doing this simple job, she's ended up with insane powers... how will she maintain her low key life now?!

IN STORES NOW!

Light Novel Volumes 1-9

Manga Volumes 1-5